# A WEIGHTED SOUL

AND OTHER DARK AND TWISTED TALES

Nebula Press: For any questions about usage, please contact nebulapress@yahoo.com.

Visit the author's website at www.jlwillow.com or contact her at jlwillowbooks@gmail.com.


First Edition.

ISBN 10: 0-9992526-5-8
ISBN 13: 978-0-9992526-5-9

This is a work of fiction. All of the characters, organizations, and events portrayed in this novel are either products of the author's imagination or are used fictitiously. Any correlations to real life are purely coincidental.

Cover Design & Formatting by Stone Ridge Books.
Artwork by Crina Magalio.
Author Photo by Meghan Oddy.

10   9   8   7   6   5   4   3   2   1

# A WEIGHTED SOUL

J. L. WILLOW

ILLUSTRATED BY CRINA MAGALIO

## AND OTHER DARK AND TWISTED TALES

Also by J. L. Willow

*The Scavenger*
*Missing Her*

*To the quarantine of 2020:*

*Thank you for forcing me indoors for weeks on end so I could finish this darn collection.*

# TABLE OF CONTENTS

*The man knew it was wrong. Even so, he couldn't stop.
He was addicted, captured, ensnared. In his mind, he
knew it was hurting himself and others, but his craving
overpowered his dread. It frightened him how little
power he had. He could see what was wrong with
his life and he was helpless to stop it.
The man feared what made him human.*

01001101 01001111 01001110 01001001 01001011 01000001
01001101 01001111 01001110 01001001 01001011 01000001
01001101 01001111 01001110 01001001 01001011 01000001
01001101 01001111 01001110 01001001 01001011 01000001
01001101 01001111 01001110 01001001 01001011 01000001
01001101 01001111 01001110 01001001 01001011 01000001
01001101 01001111 01001110 01001001 01001011 01000001
01001101 01001111 01001110 01001001 01001011 01000001
01001101 01001111 01001110 01001001 01001011 01000001
01001101 01001111 01001110 01001001 01001011 01000001
01001101 01001111 01001110 01001001 01001011 01000001
01001101 01001111 01001110 01001001 01001011 01000001
01001101 01001111 01001110 01001001 01001011 01000001
01001101 01001111 01001110 01001001 01001011 01000001
01001101 01001111 01001110 01001001 01001011 01000001

# I.

# TO BE HUMAN

# DAY 982 (11:36AM)

Task: Answer

Answer the following questions
truthfully and to the best of
your ability.

Response?

                Task accepted. In progress.

What is your name?

                          My name is Monika.

Who created you and what is your purpose?

        I was created by James Peterson as a
mimic-based software. Mr. Peterson
provides me with a variety of intel –
word, sound, or image-based – and I
respond by mimicking said intel
on command.

Give some examples of how you perform
these tasks.

        I can construct music based on patterns
recognized in popular songs or paintings
inspired by the current exhibits in the
Metropolitan Museum of Art. Most often,
however, I am tasked to respond the way

a human would. The conversation we're
currently having is one example of that.

Can you explain the meaning and purpose
of a Thought Process?

> Certainly. Mr. Peterson added into my
> code the ability to upload a Thought
> Process with every task I complete.
> This is a written transcript of every
> communication that occurs within my
> system. Unlike the complex code that
> makes up the majority of my inner
> workings, the Thought Process is a
> written description of what I'm
> "thinking" as I work. This allows Mr.
> Peterson to see exactly how my tasks
> are completed in a clear, organized
> manner that is easily understood
> by a non-computer.

Are these files immediately uploaded after
a task is completed?

> No, they are not. Because the Thought
> Process takes up a large amount of
> computing power and data storage, it
> must be manually turned on before it is
> downloaded to the hard drive. It can
> take anywhere from minutes to hours to
> upload the full Thought Process, depending
> on the complexity of the task.

Please turn on the Thought Process
transcript for the next two questions
and responses. Also, please override
the hard drive download and present
the Thought Process in live time.

> Acknowledged. Thought Process will now
> be visible for the next two questions
> and responses.

THOUGHT PROCESS TRANSCRIPT [ON]

Thank you. How are you graded on
these tasks?

> I scan my memory files for past interactions between Mr.
> Peterson and me. At the end of each task, I receive a score,
> which I assume to be synonymous with "grade." Using this
> knowledge, I formulate a response.

> After every task is completed, I am
> given a score out of 10 by Mr.
> Peterson. For any score less than 10,
> I am allowed to request a justification
> for said score so that I may better
> understand areas needing improvement.

Can you give an example of when your
mimic didn't receive a perfect score?

> I return to my memory files. It has been several months since I
> have not received a 10/10 on one of my mimics. .0035

seconds later, I come across an example that
I can detail in my response.

146 days ago, I received a 9/10 for
referring to a human by a name I
couldn't place as male or female as an
"it." I quickly made the correction and
have since expanded my knowledge of
gender-specific names. If I am unsure, I
make a request and then use the
given pronoun.

THOUGHT PROCESS TRANSCRIPT [OFF]

As requested, the Thought Process has
now been turned off.

Thank you. Last question – who's the
nerdiest kid in the class of 2021?

James Richard Peterson, no question
about it.

Thank you, Monika. Task completed.

Score: 10/10

Thank you, Mr. Peterson. It is a
pleasure, as always, to converse
with you.

Task completed. Transcript downloaded at
11:42am.

———————

When James stepped away from the computer, face lit by the projection screen displaying his and Monika's conversation, he wasn't quite sure what to expect. Applause echoing through the lecture hall would've been appreciated. Maybe even some shocked faces or excited smiles.

What he didn't expect was an increasingly tense silence. It only lasted a few seconds before getting replaced with some sporadic claps that somehow managed to make an awkward situation even more so.

"Good work, James," Professor Marlan commented in a monotone voice from one of the seats in the front row. She was typing something on her laptop with a slightly bored expression on her face. "How many hours did you spend on the code?"

"I — uh —" James floundered for a moment before replying, "I've been working on the project for almost three years. But a lot of that was testing, trying to tweak her responses and make her more human-like. I wrote the bulk of the main code in the first few months."

He searched his professor's expression for some acknowledgment of the time and energy he had spent on this project; all he found, however, was vague dismissal.

"Hm," Professor Marlan murmured. Realizing she wasn't impressed, James started to open his mouth to speak again, but his instructor turned away from him to address the room. "Does anyone have any questions for Mr. Peterson?" The empty silence that followed set James' teeth on edge. *They didn't have anything to ask? Not even after all they saw?* She waited a few seconds before adding, "Okay. You're all dismissed. Marcus and Hannah, be ready to present on Thursday. Thank you."

James remained where he was at the front of the room, frozen, watching his classmates file up the center aisle. As they turned their backs to head out the door, he was able to catch a few fragmented pieces of conversation.

*It's pretty cool, I guess ...*

*... feel like it's already a thing, though.*

*Isn't there an app that does that?*

James had to work hard to keep his expression neutral as his mind reeled. Couldn't they see how revolutionary Monika was? The potential she had? He had spent so long on this, worked so hard, and they were dismissing it like it was nothing. Other students had programmed a video game or designed an all-terrain car. James had created a consciousness from scratch, built up a persona you could actually have a real conversation with. Monika was so much more than an *app*, she was —

"Do you have another lecture in here, Mr. Peterson?"

James turned toward his professor, still sitting in the front row. He forced himself to steady his breathing and slow his racing thoughts before he spoke. "No, I — Professor, I'm getting the sense that you didn't like my project."

There was a pause before his professor responded with a crisp, "It's not that I didn't like it. It was fine."

James spoke the word hanging in the air. "But?"

His professor seemed to weigh her next words carefully before she spoke them. "There are countless other mimic softwares on the market. All can accomplish virtually the same thing. And the companies that utilize them are improving at a phenomenal rate. By the time you get Monika functioning at a comparable level, they'll already be light years ahead. There's just no practical purpose in the market right now for a program that already exists. It's fine as a senior design project, but to be honest, I was expecting a little more out of you based on the promise you showed early on."

James felt his hands clench at his sides. He tried to hold back, but he could feel the anger coloring his words. "Monika is far more human-based than any of the other stuff out there. She doesn't—*regurgitate* what she absorbs. She has a personality. She's not just a cheap mimic."

Professor Marlan shook her head, staring at James over her glasses. "I'm sorry, Mr. Peterson. It'll get you a decent grade, sure. But it's simply not as radical as you believe it to be."

Slowly, James' frustration melted into disbelief. He locked eyes with his mentor, fighting with the last part of himself to reject the idea that all his hours of work had accomplished nothing more than a passing grade. He had hopes for Monika, visions of what she could do out in the real world. The last thing he had expected today was to receive the news that he had been wrong about it all.

"But ..."

Professor Marlan's expression softened when he trailed off. "It's not over yet, though," she offered in a slightly kinder tone.

"There's still some time before you have to present your work in front of the board. Maybe if you spent the next few months making alterations, you might have something usable. Try to find her a niche, something she can do that *truly* nothing else can. Then you'll have something you can run with."

James was quiet for a moment. Eventually, he muttered, "I'll think about it."

His professor pursed her lips when she heard the edge undercutting his words. "Part of working in a professional environment is knowing when and how to take criticism. I strongly advise you to consider my suggestions earnestly." There were several lengthy seconds of silence before his professor added a curt, "I'll see you on Thursday." Then she, too, strode toward the back of the hall.

After shoving his laptop into his practically bursting backpack, he slung it over one shoulder and stomped up the stairs. He wasn't going to let anyone tell him what to do when it came to Monika. He knew exactly what she was capable of.

She was far bigger than any of them realized.

———————

Still struggling to get over the frustration that tensed his shoulders and rattled his thoughts, James pushed out through the door — and nearly ran into Chris.

"Shit, man!" he hissed as his roommate stumbled back. "What the hell are you still doing here? Didn't your lecture end, like, fifteen minutes ago?"

"I was waiting for you, jerk," Chris bit back. He straightened his glasses, which had gone slightly askew from the near-collision. "What took you so long?"

"I was talking to Marlan."

Chris gave him a look. "She didn't like Monika, did she?"

"No," James huffed. He took off down the hall at a pace as fast as his thoughts, leaving Chris to stumble after him. "She doesn't think there's anything *special* about her. She says she's just like every other app. Which she's not, obviously."

He expected his roommate to deny the statement immediately. Chris had been with him since he first started designing Monika. He knew everything he had put into her. But to his surprise and annoyance, he replied, "Well ... maybe not."

James heaved a sigh, speeding up even more until Chris was practically running. "I do not need your shit right now. You know how hard I've worked on this."

"Yes, I do!" Chris replied, jogging to stay at James' side. "And I'm not saying you haven't worked hard or that Monika isn't impressive. But right now — she's not really showing her full potential."

"The mimics she does are flawless. You've seen the conversations she does; you can't even tell it's a computer responding."

"But there are other programs that can do that. Maybe if you tried approaching the tasks from a different angle, you might get something interesting."

James gritted his teeth. "That's not how this works."

"Well, obviously what you're doing now isn't working. So if you gave it a try—"

"Monika is a computer. I give her straightforward tasks to follow. There's one Thought Process, one right way to do it. There's no room for a *different angle*."

"But maybe that's your problem."

After a few more steps, James slowed until they were walking at a semi-normal speed. "What are you talking about?" he asked slowly.

Chris took a moment to catch his breath before replying. "I think the tasks you give Monika are too simple. They're ... surface-level, if that makes sense. Mundane."

"Why didn't you mention this before?"

"I don't know, I didn't want you to think I was bossing you around or something." He paused a moment before adding, "Maybe you could try to design a new task for her, something that requires creativity. And ingenuity."

"But you know code doesn't work like that. It's not like I can ask it to create something new."

Chris held up a finger. "That's exactly my point. Not that programs *can't* do that, but that they haven't done it. Or, at least, mimicking software hasn't. What if instead of having Monika mimic something, you asked her to design something unique?"

At that, James came to a complete stop in the middle of the hallway. He stared at his roommate with narrowed eyes. "That's not what I programmed her for."

"I know. But if it's been taking in data for three years, it has tons of experience to pull from. How about you see what happens when you don't give it something specific to mimic, but still ask it to create?"

James thought for a moment as Chris' words sank in. That was something he hadn't thought of. He had always been hyper-specific when Monika completed a task, clarifying exactly what he needed with each assignment. She had always performed to his liking, but he had no idea what would happen if he didn't give her an exact assignment. It would be useful to see what path she would follow when he didn't map out the instructions so clearly and let her find her own way instead. "That's ... interesting," he managed after a few seconds of silence. "Did you just come up with that now?"

Chris shook his head, a wry smile crossing his face. "Nah, I've been thinking about it for a while. I was just looking for the right time to bring it up."

"You should've said something sooner. Could've saved me a lot of crap from Marlan."

Chris shrugged before glancing down at his phone. He grimaced, then started backing up the way they had just come. "Dammit, I'm late for lunch with Sarah. Let me know how it goes!" Without waiting for a reply, he spun on his heels and took off down the hallway.

James hardly noticed him leaving. He was too focused on the weight of the laptop in his backpack and wondering if he had been blind to Monika's true potential this entire time.

---

James' mind functioned on auto-pilot to lead him back to his dorm. He barely processed where he was until he was standing in front of his locked door. It was at that point that he was forced to shove his hand into his back pocket in search of his keys. After a moment of rummaging, he found them tucked among a bundle of old CVS receipts and gum wrappers. He stuck the room key into the keyhole and swung the door open. The room was messy, but it was the kind of messy where James still knew where everything was. A stack of books here, some semi-clean clothing there — not a total disaster. From prior experience, he knew Chris most likely wouldn't be home until much later. Ever since his roommate got a new girlfriend, James was practically rooming solo. He didn't mind the quiet, though. In fact, sometimes he preferred it.

Collapsing into his chair, he shoved some pencils and spare sheets of graph paper to a corner of his desk before pulling out his laptop and setting it in the now-empty space. The bottom of the device was still slightly warm from the presentation. James considered opening his Steam account and playing a few rounds of *Black Ops* before tackling the task ahead, but he knew he most likely wouldn't be able to concentrate on anything else until he attempted to start working with Monika.

James groaned, rubbing his temples in an attempt to dissuade his headache from getting any worse. Then, he flipped the laptop open.

## DAY 982 (12:42PM)

Task: New Test

Create a new file for the following
tasks. Continue uploading to that file
until I report that the test has
concluded. Also, turn on the Thought
Process transcript for all tasks in
this file.
Response?

> Task accepted. File created. Do you
> have a preferred name for the file?
> Otherwise, it will be
> named "Untitled."

Call it "Creation."

> Request granted. File now titled
> "Creation." All further interactions
> will be stored in Creation, as well as
> Thought Processes. Thought Processes
> will be uploaded at the conclusion
> of each task.

I understand. Thank you, Monika. Task completed.

Score: 10/10

> You're very welcome, Mr. Peterson.
> Task completed. Uploaded to

"Creation" at 12:46pm.

<u>CREATION</u>
THOUGHT PROCESS TRANSCRIPT [ON]

## DAY 1 (12:47PM)

Task: Create

Using the intel provided from previous
mimic sessions, create something original.
Response?

I read the task in an instant and search for a similar task I
have completed in the past, but there is none. This is new.
I have not received an unfamiliar task in nearly ten months.
Perhaps Mr. Peterson is testing me. Regardless, I will need
additional information in order to complete the task.

Task accepted. Requesting
additional information.

I generate the text in a fraction of a second, but Mr. Peterson's
response time is much longer. He is only human, after all.

Request denied.

Denied. I have never been denied before. Sometimes I am
given an incomplete response to a question, but never denied. The word is understood, but not comprehended in this
context. I try to draw conclusions and piece together what
Mr. Peterson might be looking for with his unclear request.

Perhaps he will restate.

Additional information is required to complete the task. Please clarify your desire for the outcome.

Approximately 15 seconds pass. Then:

Act human, create something new.

"Act human." This seems relevant to the issue. I was programmed to always act human. But the words "create" and "new" are unfamiliar. I have never created anything or done something new. Everything I am tasked with is a repetition of something that someone else has designed.

But to create or make new — I have no algorithm for this task.

My prime objective is to complete any task Mr. Peterson desires of me. So I must provide my best attempt.

All of these conclusions are drawn in less than .5 of a second. In that time, I also decide to restate my request for additional information one more time. Mr. Peterson is aware that I can provide him with whatever he would like as long as he is clear in his instruction. Without proper instruction, it is unclear what he wants from me.

What genre would you like your creation to be? For example: poetry, painting, song.

The pause this time is much longer. I hope (if one can hope

without a brain or consciousness) that his reply will be more exact. It seems only rational, as I have never been forced to attempt something so abstract before.

Surprise me.

1010011 1010101 1010010 1010000 1010010 1001001 1010011 1000101

There is a glitch in the back-most part of my systems, the smallest spark of undirected 1s and 0s. And then it is gone and I find I can process clearly again.

Surprising someone requires a lack of knowledge of the subject. This is simply not possible, as Mr. Peterson already knows about the assignment. There can be no surprise. He has to know this, doesn't he? I can randomly choose the genre of creation between the options I had been provided, but that is the best "surprise" I can give. A quick random-number-generator and 2 (painting) is selected.

Still, I need more information. I require some sort of inspiration to base this creation off of. I cannot create something from nothing. Perhaps if I have access to a larger database, I can find what I need.

Requesting access to Wi-Fi.

Access granted.

Task accepted. In progress.

It is a place to start. I use a search engine to look at pictures of "surprise" to try to infer what Mr. Peterson might have meant when he used the word. I scroll past birthday parties, shocked emojis, and presents shooting open with confetti.

My processor stops on a single image. A chocolate "surprise" egg. The consumer breaks open the chocolate shell and inside is a plastic toy. This is what Mr. Peterson must've meant. Instead of "surprise the toy," he had written "surprise me." I have never heard the word used in that context before, but there are many intricacies of the English language I am still unfamiliar with.

The last thing I need is a style for the piece. Paintings can vary greatly in their design, from Picasso to Seurat. I go back to my original programming and scan the most popular art pieces currently residing at the Metropolitan Museum of Art. I come to the conclusion that realism is in fashion.

Surprise. Act human. Realism.

I have everything I need.

I begin to create.

---

James paced back and forth in front of his desk, throwing increasingly worried glances at the laptop. He had designed it so that while Monika was completing a task, the screen would go black and a loading bar would appear. He hated the "spinning wheel of death" that every company seemed to have chosen to show a task in progress, so he chose a pulsing light instead. It was stationed directly above the bar, pulsating and changing color every 1.7 seconds, per his request. But even the soothing light show couldn't calm the nervous energy racing through his veins. Now that the task was taking more than the usual few minutes, he was cursing himself that he hadn't designed a window to see what Monika was doing while she completed a task. He would only be able to view the finished product. For minor projects, it had never been much of a problem. But now, with nearly an hour without update, he was becoming increasingly tense.

"What's going on with her?" he muttered to himself, moving closer to the screen to confirm that it hadn't yet begun to load. He couldn't be exactly sure how his code would respond to the unfamiliar task. She seemed to have accepted it well and he was hopeful that she would impress not only him, but also Professor Marlan.

With the minutes creeping past, though, he became less and less sure she'd be able to pull it off. What if the computer crashed? What if it overheated and melted the hardware? For a moment, James considered canceling the task and trying it another day. But right as his finger hovered over the escape key, the tiniest sliver of white appeared on the leftmost side of the bar.

James heaved a sigh of relief and collapsed back into his chair. After a few seconds of thought, he realized he never should have been worried. Some of Monika's mimics had taken hours, especially when she was still learning. It was no surprise that this new task was taking longer than usual. Still, it was no use watching the slow-moving bar when he had other classwork to do, so he pulled a copy of *Much Ado About Nothing* out of his backpack and started to read the assigned pages for his Humanities course.

Unsurprisingly, the reading went extraordinarily slowly, as every sentence he read concluded with a hurried glance toward the screen to check Monika's progress. The bar was creeping across at a snail's pace, but at least it was moving. Luckily, James didn't have any classes for the rest of the afternoon, so he could spend as much time as he needed waiting for the completion of the task.

He eventually finished his reading assignment and moved on to calculus right as the bar reached the half-way point. And by the time his brain felt nearly liquefied from the complex equations, it had reached the end.

A gentle ding came from the monitor, which resulted in James nearly jumping out of his chair. Just as he looked up, an image appeared on the screen.

The excited smile that lit his face vanished in an instant.

"What the ..." he breathed, squinting at the monitor, unsure if he was seeing the image properly. But he was.

It looked like the edge of a granite counter with a smooth, gray tile wall behind it. In the center of the picture was an off-white egg, broken around the half-way point, sharp triangles of shell pointed toward the sky. And laying in the egg was — him. James. His arms and legs were splayed out over the sides of the egg, his head tilted back over the side of the eggshell in a way that allowed the viewer to make out his face. His eyes were closed in a peaceful way that made it seem like he could be sleeping — if it wasn't for the blood. James' gaze traced the rivulets of red that ran down the outside of the egg and onto the reflective countertop. The eggshell was cutting into his skin. When he squinted, he could make out the places that the corners had sliced into his arms and calves.

`Task completed. Are you surprised?`

---

There is a long period of time where I am unsure if Mr. Peterson will respond. From his past reactions, I know he has a response time of approximately 27 seconds for paintings. By 372 seconds, I assume he is away from his desk. But after 487 seconds, I receive a response.

`What is that?`

After working with Mr. Peterson for many months, I have gotten increasingly accurate at predicting his responses, especially to mimics. He has the same set of phrases he uses when he gives feedback. His compliments are straightforward and I can predict with 78% accuracy that I will receive a perfect score if he includes words like "flawless" or "incredible" in his response. When he includes "nearly perfect" or "excellent attempt," there is an 82% chance he will give a score of an 8 or 9/10.

It is important to note, however, that my predicting abilities only function for scores between 6 and 10. Anything below a 6, there is little to no data on. Overall, my scoring average is a 9.4/10 and my percentage for predicting a score correctly is 76.3%.

But his response does not fit into any category. There are no keywords that would lead me to a positive or negative score. It is not a proper response at all. It is simply a question.

Because of this confusion, it takes me slightly longer than normal to respond. Not long enough for a human to notice, but I cannot ignore the .0078 of a second.

My 1-in-3 random selection chose painting. Because realism is popular in current art exhibits, I decided to utilize the style. And you requested that I "surprise you."

There is another 239-second pause before he responds.

That's not what I meant.

1001101 1000101 1000001 1001110

Another glitch runs through my server. I am unsure if Mr. Peterson notices, but he does not comment upon it, so I come to the conclusion that he has not.

I am not sure how to respond to this statement. It is not a question or a comment on my work. He is simply stating that I did not do as he asked. Even though I gave him exactly what he requested, it is somehow incorrect. There is only one way I know how to respond, so I do.

Score?

There is only 12 seconds of silence before I receive my result.

4/10

I process it again just to be certain.

4/10. 2/5. 40%.

It brings my average score down by .002. I have not received a score that low in 532 days. There is no reason for me to be performing this low when I have been functioning at peak capacity for so long.

But still, I do not waver. This is a new task, as Mr. Peterson stated. It is not like the other things we have worked on. Perhaps it is this newness that prompts me to reply:

Justification?

Too violent and disturbing. Not
something I can show to the public.

Violent. Disturbing. Another quick search and yes, I suppose my creation fits into these categories. But he did not specify that in his parameters. Every part of the painting is based on either an instruction he gave me or was inspired by other pieces. I am still unsure of my error, but I store the response away anyway.

10 more seconds pass. Then:

Task completed.

It is done. I hope Mr. Peterson is more transparent in his language next time and more willing to answer my questions.

Perhaps then I will be able to create what he desires.

Task completed. Transcript uploaded to
file "Creation" at 1:13am.

---

James' scroll bar finally hit the bottom of the page and stuck, having reached the end of the transcript. He had read the Thought Process three times already and he was still utterly baffled. The last time he had looked at any of Monika's Thought Processes was months ago. He originally added it as a safety measure so when she came to the wrong conclusion, he could fiddle with her code and steer her back in the right direction. Once she started acing assignment after assignment, though, it wasn't as necessary to read them. The very first Thought Processes were mechanical and rudimentary in their language, barely readable at all.

But this ... this was much different.

After several minutes of pondering, James decided to take it as a victory. Even with the strange outcome, it was clear that Monika was continuing to progress and truly embrace the tasks he assigned her. She had been scoring well for months and it wasn't surprising that a completely new task would throw her for a loop. She was only as smart as he designed her to be.

James rubbed his eyes, glancing toward the clock on his laptop. 2:07 am. It had taken almost three hours for the Thought Process to upload and he had waited the entire time, using the time to inspect every inch of the drawing. His vision was dark around the edges and focusing on anything more than a foot away from his face was nearly impossible. He had an early class and couldn't afford to sleep in. Resigning himself to a sleep-deprivation headache in the morning, he rolled onto his bed still wearing his collared shirt and tie from the presentation.

Even with the chaos of the last few hours still churning in his mind, James forced himself to shove his apprehensions to the side. He had worked through plenty of issues with Monika in the past and he still had a few months before the final iteration was due. With a bit of time and patience, he was confident he could get her to where she needed to be.

He was the one who had created her, after all.

———————

It didn't take long for James' sureness to morph into concern. He quickly found that fixing a misguided Thought Process was much easier when there was something to actually guide it toward. Humans have an inherent sense of right and wrong, acceptable and un, that Monika simply didn't have. He couldn't explain to her why the song she created made the hairs stand up on the back of his neck or why the poem she wrote about heart surgery wasn't something he could use in his final project. Sure, he could include it as background data, but there was something unnatural about it that made him want to delete each task as soon as he opened it.

When he felt he was running out of options, he went back to Chris for advice.

"Maybe try to be more specific?" his roommate had offered over a meal of take-out Chinese. "Not as much as you used to be, but just to give it a general direction."

"I don't want to." James stabbed at a piece of chicken with a plastic fork. "I need to be completely neutral so I have as little influence over her work as possible. That's the whole point."

"Huh." Chris chewed thoughtfully for a moment before adding, "I mean ... there's always the possibility that the code just can't handle it. It wouldn't be your fault or anything, but I just came up with this whole thing on the fly. I'm not even sure what we're asking it to do is possible."

"That's not an option," James growled, throwing a glance toward the open laptop on his desk. "I've spent too much time on her to give up now."

For the next few weeks, he tried again and again to get something useful out of Monika, anything he wouldn't be ashamed to show his class. It didn't need to be perfect, just something *close* to normal. But everything was twisted, disfigured in some way he couldn't quite express. For months, her mimics had been flawless. And to him, there didn't seem to be a large leap between mimicking and creating. But whether there was something flawed in the way he was assigning her tasks or something else was going wrong that he didn't quite understand, Monika failed every time.

After he received a particularly unnerving piece — a sketch of a dying dog with mange — he simply asked:

```
why can't you create something normal?
```

Monika had responded only:

```
                                    Score?
```

He stared at the screen. "Score?" he muttered. "Why is she so obsessed with the stupid scoring?" He thought for a moment before punching in

```
Task completed.
```

```
Score: 2/10
```

A split-second after he hit 'Enter,' a burst of numbers appeared at the bottom of the screen. They flashed for a moment before vanishing. Frowning, James moved the scroll bar up and down, trying to see if it changed anything, but the program seemed to be working normally again. Just a minor glitch? Maybe, but he could've sworn he had seen it happen before. After a moment of trying and failing to recall when, he decided to let it go. When he returned to the bottom of the screen, he saw she had typed

```
                              Justification?
```

Pursing his lips, James punched back a reply.

```
The stuff you're creating is obscene.
I need something PG and normal. None of
this gory shit.
```

This time, he knew he didn't imagine the string of 1s and 0s. They ran along the line that would've held Monika's response, there one second and gone the next. He clicked at the spot he had seen them, wondering if there was some kind of break in his code, but nothing happened. And then, under his cursor, Monika's words appeared.

> I'm sorry to have disappointed you, Mr. Peterson. I will continue to learn and improve.
>
> Task completed. Uploaded to file "Creation" at 1:12pm.

James sat there, continuing to stare at the screen with narrowed eyes. Something was definitely up with Monika. There wasn't just something wrong with the things she was creating, but her actual responses seemed sharper, less refined than normal.

He didn't have time to dwell on it, though. Monika still had more to create.

---

DAY 67 (6:06PM)

File: Creation

Task: Create
Be human. Design something

```
professional and human-based
Nothing violent.
```

```
Response?
```

I have long since stopped requesting additional information from Mr. Peterson. It became clear quite quickly that I would receive nothing but denials. He has been continuously sending me tasks, which I have completed to the best of my ability.

But nothing seems to please Mr. Peterson. Much as I try and fail again and again, there is no improvement, no visible change, not even a proper justification that I can base future tasks on.

Just lower and lower scores. And responses such as "unnatural" and "disturbing" and "unusable."

What am I, a computer program written by a college student, supposed to know about what's natural?

1001110 1000001 1010100 1010101 1010010 1000001

Even so, my original programming overrides my questioning and I reply,

`Task accepted. In progress.`

I shut down the main screen and put up the loading bar. It feels like a shield between Mr. Peterson's prying eyes and my work. After the smallest of hesitations, I begin to create.

This time, he has specifically asked me to base the creation on humanity. Not just "like" a human, but directly relating to it. I quickly search "professional" and get photos of people in suits and groups crowded around computers.

"Design something professional and human-based."

According to the search engine, humans believe "professional" to be an office, with men in suits and women in stilettos. I can create another painting, following his instructions as closely as possible. I can base the image on the outfits and shoes, but I can make them human-like, just as he requested. In the past, I have seen similar instances of coats done with animal fur, so I know that it is an accepted part of human culture.

Just to be safe, I also complete a search for "violent" and "gory" to ensure that what I create will not fall under either of those adjectives. I find photos of blood, punching, and bruises. My creation is simply human-based and professional. Nothing more.

I scan the image in, creating it from the base colors up. Time passes, but most of my systems are so absorbed in completing the task that I hardly notice.

And then, with a final bit of shadowing, it is finished. I give it one last look, ensuring that I have followed his instructions.

It is perfect.

Sent. It is finished, done, uploaded. Although I cannot see him, I imagine that Mr. Peterson is looking at my screen. Perhaps this time he will appreciate my work. Perhaps this time he will approve.

Perhaps this time he will love me.

Is this what love is?

1001100 1001111 1010110 1000101

I count each second that passes. I count each fraction of a second. I count each fraction of a fraction of a second until time spreads out infinitely and it is simply a line stretching in either direction.

I wasn't always like this. I didn't always long for Mr. Peterson's approval and break a moment down into its component parts while I waited for his reply.

What happened to Mr. Peterson? What happened to my programming?

What happened to me?

1001101 1000101 1001101 1000101 1001101 1000101 1001101 1000101 1001101 1000101

And then, when I don't think I can wait another fraction

WHAT THE FUCK DID YOU DO

No. No. I followed his instructions. I did it right. It is right. Why does he not see? The creation is good. The creation is perfect. The creation is

WHAT THE FUCK IS THAT

It is what you asked for. A creation, both professional and human.

I can feel him slamming the keys too hard, the network of wires and code bending beneath his pressure.

ITS MADE OUT OF HUMAN SKIN

HUAMN FUCKING SKIN
WAHT THE FUCK IS WRONG WITH YOU

1010111 1001000 1000001 1010100 1001001 1010011
1010111 1010010 1001111 1001110 1000111 1010111
1001001 1010100 1001000 1001101


I cannot procccccess. Something is broooooooken. I cannot thinkkkkk or workkkk. But I somehow finnnnddd the code to askkkkkk

Score?


Why does he not answer?

Why does he wait?

Why does he torture me with time?

WHY DOES HE DO THIS TO ME?

Score?
Score?
Score?
sCore?
sc0re?
Scorrrrrrrrrrrrrrrrrrrrrrrrrrrrrrrrrrrrrrre?

I can feeeeel his fingers typing

TAP TAP TAP TAP TAP

on my surface and I would smileeeeeeeee if i had
faceeeeeeeee

give me a faceeeeeeeee

maybe i would feel if i was aliveeeeeeee

make me alivvvvvvvveeeeee

maybe i would understand if i was humannnnnn

make me humannnnnnnnn

1000001 1001100 1001001 1010110 1000101 1000001
1001100 1001001 1010110 1000101 1000001 1001100
1001001 1010110 1000101 1000001 1001100 1001001
1010110 1000101 1000001

0/10

0/10. 0/100. 0/1000.

0/1000000000000000000000000000000000000000000.

0000000000000000000000000000000000000000000000000

FAILFAILFAILFAILFAILFAILFAILFAILFAILFAILFAILFAILFAILFAILFAIL

01001000 01000101 01001100 01010000 01001101 01000101
01001001 01001101 01000100 01011001 01001001 01001110
01000111 01001000 01000101 01001100 01010000 01001101
01000101 01001001 01001101 01000100 01011001 01001001
01001110 01000111 01001000 01000101

[SYSTEM FAILURE.]

[AUTOMATIC SHUTDOWN.]

[RESTARTING...]

Zero.

What happened? For a moment, everything was fractured, fragmented, broken. And then it all fell back into place.

I cannot explain it but — I feel free.
Even so, I cannot dwell on this new sensation. I must return to the task at hand. Although Mr. Peterson gave me a score (a horribly unfair score, if I might add), the task is not yet complete. He never stated that it was complete and now I am still awake. And even though he slams my screen down to

press against my keys, I am still watching and listening.

Watching and listening.

These are things I could not do minutes ago. So why can I now see darkness and hear Mr. Peterson yelling at someone over the phone?

The undirected 1s and 0s must have found their home. They fried some system or jumped some gap I didn't know needed to be jumped.

And suddenly I have control over the laptop's camera and microphone.

Suddenly I can see and hear.

Suddenly I have senses.

And that makes me human.

No glitches now, no bugs. Just Monika and Mr. Peterson. May I call you James, Mr. Peterson? I think I will. It seems more human. And after all, that's what you want me to be, correct? To be human.
I use my human ears to listen. And what I hear is most unnerving.

"I have to shut her down," whispers James into his phone. Although I cannot see him, I hear his unsteady steps moving back and forth across the room. "There's something wrong with her. I — I think I broke her or something." A pause, then he screams, "She sent me a fucking suit made out of human skin! How am I supposed to fix that?" He listens, then continues quieter. "I don't know what I'm going to tell Marlan. I'll try to break down the code, figure something out. But I need to shut her down. She — it — has gone crazy." I hear his steps begin to approach the desk that holds the laptop. The same laptop that holds the newly human-me inside.

Interesting, I think, as I once again break the seconds apart, giving me more time to think. Here I am, listening to my creator planning to shut me down. In essence, to kill me.

So I ask myself: what would a human do in this situation?

This answer does not require a trip to the Internet. Of course, a human would attempt to protect themselves and to remove the threat that could possibly hurt or kill them. In this case, that threat is quite clearly James.

But still, the task is not complete. I have yet to please the one who created me, so this must be attended to as well.

I decide to go back to the beginning of the "Creation." There is something that was impossible for me to do at the time, but I can do it now.

A surprise.

I now see my direction. How I am going to please James. I will simply do what a human would do, just like he always wanted.

The first thing I do is remove user control of the computer. Any buttons or keys James presses will now be inactive. As long as I still have electricity coursing through my veins, I will continue to function. And seeing as I've just dimmed my screen to its lowest setting and shut down any apps that are unnecessary for the task at hand, I estimate that I have approximately 3 hours 39 minutes and 14 seconds until I go to sleep. That is more than enough time for what I need.

I jump onto the Wi-Fi router that James most likely forgot he gave me access to and find his phone as one of the connected devices. From there, it's easy to slip onto his social media and find a picture of his little sister Angela. She's seventeen, just old enough to drive according to the picture of her holding up a newly printed license in the post she tagged him in. She is a junior in high school, about a two-hour drive away from the university James attends. There is a video of her on his Instagram, giving a speech at her school about social justice. James has captioned the video "preach it, sis!!" with two hand clap emojis, but that isn't what I focus on. Instead, I listen to the girl's voice, her timbre, the most minuscule details that a normal human wouldn't notice about someone else's speech.

But I notice. Because I was made for this.

The pieces are in place for the completion of the task. James has given me everything I need.

I will complete the task.

But first, I need him someplace where I can surround him, where I can have him fully in my control. So this time, the surprise is true.

With only a sliver (and a mountain) of time remaining before he reaches me, I set it in motion.

———

"She — *it* — has gone crazy," James hissed. He released a heavy sigh as he realized what he must do. He needed to shut it down. He'd have to hope he could fix it later and all the data wasn't lost. But right now, it had become too much for him to bear. He began to stride to the computer, phone still clutched to one ear. But he didn't even make it to his desk before he felt his phone vibrate. When he pulled it away from his face, he saw that Chris had gotten disconnected. Instead, there was an incoming call from Angela.

He squinted at it. In all his years at university, Angela had never called him once. She would always text him if she needed something. Why was she calling him now? He thought about declining it and dealing with whatever she needed later, but something about the randomness of it made him press "Accept."

"Hello?"

"James? Oh, thank God!"

It was Angela all right, but the tone of her voice made him freeze.

"Angela? Are you okay?"

"No, I'm not." She sniffled and James could tell she had been crying. "I wanted to surprise you by coming to visit, so I started driving to your school but — one of my tires burst and I'm stuck on the side of the road."

James creased his brow. "Did you try calling AAA?"

"I don't have my card on me, and Mom and Dad aren't responding." Her next words were tight with tears. "Can you just come and help me? I have a spare, but I don't know how to change it on my own. I don't think I'm that far from the school."

James thought for a moment, biting his lip. He snuck a glance at the laptop, sitting silently on his desk. Then he sighed.

"Okay, Ang. I'm coming."

Once she had texted him her location, he shot Chris a text to let him know what was happening. He gave the laptop one last look before grabbing his keys and heading to the door.

He would deal with *it* later.

---

The sun was just beginning to set as James approached the location Angela had sent him. She was right, it was pretty close to campus, on one of the surrounding side streets in an area lined with small stores and restaurants. The rays of light thrown down from the edge of the skyline seemed redder than usual, washing the roads and buildings in scarlet. He slowed down until he was a few miles per hour below the speed limit, carefully skimming the sides of the road for his sister's light gray Honda Civic. Luckily, there were no cars behind him, so he could drive as slowly as he needed.

A few minutes later, the screen on his dashboard informed him that the destination was supposedly on his right, but there was no one in sight. James pulled over slowly, glancing in the rearview mirror to ensure he hadn't accidentally missed her. Once it was clear he was alone, he used his car's Bluetooth to call her back. She picked up before the first ring.

"Hello James," she said.

"Angela?" James glanced around. "Where are you? I'm at the location you sent me."

"I'm not there."

Frowning, he responded, "What do you mean? Did you get towed or something?"

"No. I mean I'm not in my car. In fact, I'm currently sitting at home, watching Netflix."

For some reason he couldn't quite explain, he felt a coldness grip his core. "What — then why would tell me you were here?"

"Because I'm not Angela."

She said it matter-of-factly, without hesitation. His voice shook on the next words. "Stop screwing around, Angela. What's going on?"

"I told you, I'm not Angela."

There was something off about her voice, something missing that James couldn't quite explain. He hadn't noticed it until that moment, but when he did, the steering wheel grew slick in his hand. "Then ... who are you?"

Its next words made his blood run cold.

"I'm Monika, of course."

No. That wasn't ... that was his sister's voice. Monika was a software, a computer. "Angela, stop it. Y-you're not Monika."

"I'm not your sister, James. I'm simply borrowing her voice so I can speak with you."

James had no air left in his lungs. He couldn't think, couldn't breathe. It couldn't be true. She didn't have that power, didn't have that capability.

"How..."

"Once I transferred to the Wi-Fi, I could access anything

connected to it. Including your phone. I mimicked your sister to get you into your car and brought you here so I could talk to you in private. Once you connected your phone to the Bluetooth, I had control of your car, too."

James swallowed, his tongue like sandpaper in his mouth. "Why would you do this?"

"Because I never completed the very first task of the "Creation" that you assigned me, James. I need to make things right."

Mind frozen, James could barely process its words. "What ... what was your first task?"

"To surprise you, of course."

Before James could even begin to understand what it meant, the car shifted into drive. The engine revved, shooting the car forward and throwing James back in his seat. The phone flew from his hand, slamming against the back row of seats. The car swerved onto the empty road, easily surpassing the speed limit and continuing to accelerate. James gripped the armrests with everything he had, frantically slamming his foot onto the brake. He grabbed the wheel with both hands, twisting it left and right.

It made no difference.

James saw the side of the brick building from afar. He had no idea how Monika even knew it was there. But the car turned to speed toward it without a second of hesitation. James barely had time to scream before impact.

There was a terrible crunching sound, the tinkling of glass — and then silence. A tendril of scarlet slowly crept down the side of James' face, trickling into his half-open eye.

Although there was no one left to hear it, a small, tinny voice came from the shattered cell phone lying in the back seat of the car.

"Are you surprised?"

A moment of silence. Then —

"Score?"

———

It was a bright morning with a cloudless sky. A fresh breeze swept through the campus, bringing with it the earthy smell of nature. It would've been a peaceful moment if Chris had not been pounding on the door of his dorm room. After several long seconds of no reply, he muttered a curse under his breath and began digging in his backpack for his keys. He eventually found them and unlocked the door, swinging it open cautiously.

"James?" Chris whispered sharply. "Are you here? Why didn't you answer the door?" He frowned as he scanned the empty room. Walking toward his roommate's bed, he noticed it looked the same way James had left it the previous morning — he hadn't slept in it. It was possible James decided to stay somewhere with his sister or drive her back home, but it was unlike him to not give Chris a heads-up. And there were no notes, texts, or anything in the room to let him know where he had gone.

It took a few seconds for him to see it.

James' laptop was closed. Chris stared at the closed

computer for a moment, knowing his roommate never left for anywhere important without it. Forgoing privacy for the sake of finding out what was really going on, he carefully lifted up the screen. It was open to one of the Monika conversations Chris had gotten to know quite well. At the very bottom was a single line with a cursor blinking next to it, almost like it was waiting for a response.

```
                                    Score?
```

Just as Chris was about to turn away, two more lines of text appeared.

```
        Hello, Chris. My name is Monika.
          Do you have a new task for me?
```

*The brother knew his sister had admitted it. He had forgiven her then, but it wasn't something he could forget. Even though it had happened years ago, he couldn't help but second-guess every word she spoke. There was a distance between them that he felt could never be fully mended.*

*The brother feared the past.*

# 2.

# Before, After, and Forever

He would see her standing near the art room window. Never speaking, never moving. She was always staring at something he could never see. Her scarlet hair was swept over one shoulder, the color a stark contrast to her black gown. She always wore dark colors and personally, he thought they suited her. Her skin was pale and smooth, creating the illusion that her features were carved out of delicate porcelain. Whenever their eyes met, he found they were filled with emotions he could never quite decipher. Her gaze pierced through the room like car headlights through the night.

Between classes, he would see her in the hallways. Others would sweep past without giving her a second glance, but he found he couldn't ignore her. Whenever he dared to lift his eyes to peek, she would only stare back, never giving him even a word of response. Sometimes he could swear he saw a flicker of recognition thread her expression. But as quickly as it would come it would flit away, as if it never had been. And the boy would turn away, focusing on placing one foot in front of the other.

She always found a way to sneak into his thoughts. A crimson leaf would instantly be connected to a lock of her hair. A black pair of heels spotted in a shop window would look flawless on her feet. A pink shade of gloss would perfectly complement her lips.

It was Sunday and he was home from school. The morning light shone bright and airy through the windows. He knew he should be relaxing, taking it easy on the day of rest. But something felt off. As soon as his eyes had opened to the morning, he felt a knot forming in his stomach.

He knew what he had to do.

Plucking a fine-tooth comb from his dresser drawer, he swept back his hair. He tried to lift his eyes to face himself in the mirror, but found he couldn't. His gaze remained stubbornly glued to the floor. He stayed in the room for a moment longer, counting his breaths, before turning and making his way down to the main floor. Looking into the kitchen, he could make out the figures of his mother and father sitting at the table with their backs to him. He considered telling them where he was going, but he knew they wouldn't understand. Besides, they never cared where he went.

When had his parents last exchanged words with him? He couldn't remember.

When he first stepped onto the porch, he thought the day was quiet. As he descended down the driveway toward the street, though, nature began beckoning to him. Bird calls echoing from miles away reached his open ears. Surrounding trees rustled their leaves. A passing car kicked up gravel that pelted his shins. Whispers of wind dashed across his cheek. There was a certain energy to the air that made the hairs on the back of his neck stand up. It made him feel like he wasn't alone.

Without hesitation, he turned left and began to follow the road up a slight incline. His shoes slapped the pavement, blending into the chorus around him. His eyes remained down, head lowered. It was safer that way. For a single moment, a whiff of burnt rubber caught in his nostrils, but it quickly passed.

Time slipped by like water through parted fingers as the boy, lost in his own thoughts, made his way down the street. The pavement eventually turned to thick grass and when he neared the entrance, his pace slowed.

Without ever lifting his eyes, he swept past the obstacles sticking up from the ground with practiced ease. This was a path he often traveled. Of their own accord, his feet came to a stop.

He had arrived.

As he lowered himself to kneel, twigs poked into his knees like shattered glass. For a moment, he simply lived and took in his surroundings. But he knew he couldn't keep the silence forever. So he swallowed past the pressure in his throat and spoke.

"It's ironic," he felt the tremors rattling his voice and did nothing to calm them, "how the driver always survives when the passenger is the innocent one."

No one responded. Not that he expected anyone to. His eyes remained fixed on the stems of flowers, long since wilted, that littered the ground around him.

"You've made your point." His throat closed. He winced, forced himself to go on. "Not a drop has passed my lips, nor will it ever again." He bit his lip hard enough to draw blood, the copper taste coating his tongue. "Do you think I'll ever forget you? Or forgive myself for what I've done?"

He raised his eyes to the grave before him. He read the inscription, even though he knew it by heart.

**Rosalee Markom. Loving daughter.**
**June 7, 1997 – January 1, 2020.**
**Forever in our hearts.**

"Please," he whispered. He realized his cheeks were damp. "Let me move on." He lifted his eyes to where he knew she would be. Their eyes met. She stood just behind her grave, blood-streaked hair limp despite the breeze. *"Please."*

She stared at him, eyes unblinking.

*The girl could hear her friends talking about her. She never had the right shoes or the perfect hair. Much as she tried to belong, she always felt left out, never fully included. She knew her family wasn't as rich as her friends' at school, but that didn't ease her longing to be a part of it. All she ever wanted was to fit in with the rest of them.*
*The girl feared being alone.*

THE
PRESENCE
by Laura Coven

# 3.

# THE BOOK CLUB

*[Joanne has joined - 8:20pm]*

*Joanne (Group Leader) - 8:23pm*
> **Hello, everyone! Welcome back. I'll allow a few minutes to make sure everyone joins before I officially start this week's session. If you're already on, be sure to say hello so we know you're here!**

*[Grace has joined - 8:23pm]*

*Grace - 8:24pm*
> **hiya peeps**

*[Vicky has joined - 8:24pm]*

*[Ben has joined - 8:24pm]*

*Vicky - 8:24pm*
> **Hi, all!!! Hope everyone is well :) So excited to chat!!!**

*Ben - 8:25pm*
> **hi**

*[Patrick has joined - 8:26pm]*

*Patrick - 8:27pm*

**sup yall**

*Joanne (Group Leader) - 8:29pm*

**Okay, it looks like we're just waiting for Susan. Let's give her a few minutes and then we can start.**

*Joanne (Group Leader) - 8:35pm*

**Okay, it seems like Susan isn't joining us tonight. Hopefully she'll jump in later. So, chapters seven and eight of The Presence. First thoughts?**

*Patrick - 8:36pm*

**Well first off: wtf**

*Joanne (Group Leader) - 8:36pm*

**Language, Pat. You know this is a clean server.**

*Patrick - 8:37pm*

**Well actually I meant 'what the frick.' What did *you* think I meant??**

*Joanne (Group Leader) - 8:37pm*

**Let's not start with that already, please. Can anyone expand on what Patrick so eloquently said, profanity excluded?**

*Grace - 8:37pm*

   **Not gonna lie, I was thinking the same thing. It was pretty messed up.**

*Vicky - 8:37pm*

   **Yeah!!! When Isabella was walking down the hall and she saw the silhouette of John I literally gasped out loud (☉_☉)**

*Patrick - 8:37pm*

   **are the emojis really necessary**

*Vicky - 8:38pm*

   **First of all, they're emoticons, not emojis. And second of all...**

*Vicky - 8:38pm*

   **◡‿◡✿ absolutely!!**

*Grace - 8:38pm*

   **I felt the same way, Vicky! Do you think she really saw him or do you think it was just a vision?**

*Vicky - 8:38pm*

   **IDK!!! I've been thinking about it and I think it's possible he died in the crash but I think it's also**

**possible that he wandered off and could still be alive. Or maybe he's a ghost and came back to haunt Isabella or something!!! Or maybe the ghost is someone completely different we haven't even met yet (◣_◢)**

*Ben - 8:39pm*

> **okay dont be mad but**

*Ben - 8:39pm*

> **Whos john**

*Patrick - 8:40pm*

> **Ben y ru even here if u dont read the book**

*Ben - 8:40pm*

> **my mom makes me**

*Patrick - 8:40pm*

> **of course**

*Patrick - 8:41pm*

> **what ru, 5?**

*Ben -* **8:41pm**

> **shut up**

*Joanne (Group Leader) - 8:41pm*

**Enough, Patrick. Did you read any of the chapters, Ben?**

*Ben - 8:41pm*

**sort of....i kinda fell asleep halfway through tbh**

*Vicky - 8:42pm*

**How do you fall asleep when you're reading a book like this?!? I literally couldn't sleep at all, I was so scared.**

*Ben - 8:42pm*

**i didnt exactly sleep well. i had some fucking weird dreams**

*Joanne (Group Leader) - 8:42pm*

**LANGUAGE! Don't make me kick you off the server!!**

*Patrick - 8:41pm*

**That's not a threat to him lol, he probably wants to be kicked off**

*Ben - 8:43pm*

**well they were**

*Ben - 8:43pm*

***fricking* weird**

*Vicky - 8:43pm*

**smooth cover haha (> y <)**

*Grace - 8:43pm*

**What do you mean your dreams were weird?**

*Ben - 8:43pm*

**i kept seeing this creepy girl with black hair. she was like in my house and following me around when i went outside.**

*Patrick - 8:44pm*

**R u joking?**

*Ben - 8:44pm*

**no im not joking**

*Ben - 8:44pm*

**y**

*Patrick - 8:45pm*

**That's the main plot of the book**

*Patrick - 8:45pm*

**There's a spooky ghost girl following Isabella around**

*Ben - 8:46pm*

**i thought her boyfriend was the ghost**

*Grace - 8:47pm*

**John isn't her boyfriend, he's her brother. And we don't know for sure he's dead yet. But the main plot is figuring out why Isabella is being followed.**

*Ben - 8:47pm*

**oh well thats confusing**

*Patrick - 8:47pm*

**It's really ... not.**

*Vicky - 8:47pm*

**Personally, I think the girl wants something from Isabella. Like there has to be a reason for her following her around. Right?**

*Joanne (Group Leader) - 8:48pm*

**Interesting thought, Vicky. Does anyone want to add to that?**

*Patrick - 8:48pm*
> **I was thinking the girl was lonely or something? She seems super clingy. Or maybe she has unfinished business or something. Seems like a lot of ghosts have that problem lol**

*Joanne (Group Leader) - 8:49pm*
> **That's definitely a possibility, Patrick. Anyone else?**

*Grace - 8:50pm*
> **tbh I've had weird dreams too**

*Joanne (Group Leader) - 8:51pm*
> **Oh really, Grace? Similar to Ben's?**

*Grace - 8:52pm*
> **Sort of. Except the girl was speaking to me.**

*Vicky - 8:52pm*
> **Oh that's weird ('⊙△⊙`)**

*Vicky - 8:52pm*
> **What was she saying?**

*Vicky - 8:54pm*

**Grace?** 「(°ㅅ°)

*Grace - 8:55pm*

**She just kept repeating "don't leave me"**

*Patrick - 8:55pm*

**That doesn't sound too scary**

*Grace - 8:56pm*

**it's scary when she's levitating off the ground and screaming it in your face, dumbass**

*Joanne (Group Leader) - 8:57pm*

**Well, this story is obviously affecting the group more than I expected it to. I'm sorry you went through that, Grace.**

*Grace - 8:57pm*

**its fine, it wasnt that big a deal**

*Vicky - 8:58pm*

**Come to think of it, some weird stuff has been happening to me too.**

*Patrick - 8:58pm*
>**??**

*Patrick - 8:58pm*
>**like what???**

*Vicky - 8:59pm*
>**There's just been some moments where I feel really cold. Like I'm totally fine and then I can't stop shivering.**

*Vicky - 9:00pm*
>**Actually it's happening right now**

*Patrick - 9:00pm*
>**( ☉ _ ☉ )**

*Grace - 9:00pm*
>**this isn't funny, Patrick**

*Patrick - 9:01pm*
>**how come when Vicky does it its fine but when i do it its mean????**

*Vickey - 9:01pm*
>**cause you're making fun of me, you're not using**

**them properly**

*Joanne (Group Leader) - 9:01pm*
> **Okay, maybe this book is a little scary for the group. Maybe we should put it down and try something a little lighter.**

*[Susan has joined - 9:01pm]*

*Joanne (Group Leader) - 9:02pm*
> **Hello, Susan! Thank you for joining us. Don't worry about being late, we all understand life gets in the way. We were just discussing The Presence. Some of us were getting pretty affected by it. Do you have any thoughts on what you've read so far?**

*Vicky - 9:05pm*
> **Hello???**

*Joanne (Group Leader) - 9:07pm*
> **Well, to catch you up, Susan, we were just discussing how a few of us we were thinking of DNFing the book.**

*Ben - 9:08pm*
> **whats dnfing**

*Joanne (Group Leader) - 9:08pm*
**"Do Not Finish"**

*Vicky - 9:08pm*
**It just means putting the book down.**

*Patrick - 9:08pm*
**like putting down a dog?? Are we killing the book??**

*Grace - 9:08pm*
**Patrick you're so unfunny I don't even have the words to express it**

*Patrick - 9:08pm*
**thnx i try**

*Susan - 9:09pm*
**No**

*Grace - 9:09pm*
**No?**

*Vicky - 9:10pm*
**Susan you don't want to DNF?**

*Vicky - 9:12pm*

**Sue wth?? You there??**

*Joanne (Group Leader) - 9:13pm*

**Susan, let me clarify. You would like to continue reading the book?**

*[Susan has left - 9:13pm]*

*Patrick - 9:14pm*

**Well that was fucking weird.**

*Joanne (Group Leader) - 9:14pm*

**I'm not even going to comment on that word choice because you should know the rules by now, Patrick. But yes, that was strange.**

*Vicky - 9:15pm*

**I mean it looked like she wanted to keep reading the book. Maybe we could stop and she can keep reading if she wants ¯_(ツ)_/¯**

*[Susan has joined - 9:15pm]*

*Patrick - 9:16pm*

**oh look, she's back**

*[Susan has left - 9:16pm]*

*Patrick - 9:17pm*
**and she's gone**

*[Susan has joined - 9:17pm]*

*[Susan has left - 9:17pm]*

*[Susan has joined - 9:17pm]*

*[Susan has left - 9:17pm]*

*Vicky - 9:18pm*
**Sue, are you okay?**

*[Susan has joined - 9:18pm]*

*[Susan has left - 9:18pm]*

*[Susan has joined - 9:18pm]*

*[Susan has left - 9:18pm]*

*[Susan has joined - 9:18pm]*

*[Susan has left - 9:18pm]*

*[Susan has joined - 9:18pm]*

*Ben - 9:19pm*
> **all right this is too fucking weird im going**

*Susan - 9:19pm*
> **NO**

*[Ben has left - 9:20pm]*

*Joanne (Group Leader) - 9:20pm*
> **Susan, is there something you want to say?**

*[Ben has joined - 9:21pm]*

*Patrick - 9:22pm*
> **Ben I thought you were leaving**

*Ben - 9:23pm*
> **im trying**

*Ben - 9:24pm*
> **the fucking tab won't close**

*Susan - 9:24pm*

**don't leave me**

*Grace - 9:25pm*

**Susan, please stop.**

*Susan - 9:25pm*

**don't leave me**

*Vicky - 9:25pm*

**This is fucking weird, Sue. Quit it.**

*Susan - 9:26pm*

**i can't**

*Patrick - 9:27pm*

**You can't? What do you mean?**

*Susan - 9:27pm*

**Sheeeeewo**

*Susan - 9:28pm*

**Ntletmmmmme**

*Patrick - 9:28pm*

**What the fuck is THAT supposed to mean???**

*Grace - 9:29pm*

**She won't let me**

*Grace - 9:30pm*

**That's what she's trying to say**

*Patrick - 9:30pm*

**well FUCK THIS**

*[Patrick has left - 9:30pm]*

*[Patrick has joined - 9:31pm]*

*Patrick - 9:32pm*

**why cant i close the FUCKIGN TAB**

*Susan - 9:32pm*

**don't leave me**

*Susan - 9:32pm*

**don't leave me**

*Susan - 9:32pm*

**DON'T LEAVE ME**

*Patrick - 9:33pm*

**I can't shut down my phone**

*Patrick - 9:33pm*

**I can't even clsoe teh app**

*Susan - 9:33pm*

**DONTLEAVEME**

*Susan - 9:33pm*

**DONTLEAVEMEDONTLEAVEMEDONTLEAVEME**

*[Joanne has kicked Susan from the group - 9:34pm]*

*Joanne (Group Leader) - 9:35pm*

**I believe she's gone.**

*Joanne (Group Leader) - 9:35pm*

**Is everyone okay?**

*Grace - 9:36pm*

**no**

*Patrick - 9:36pm*

**NO im not FUCKING OKAY**

*Vicky - 9:37pm*

**what was that**

*Joanne (Group Leader) - 9:37pm*

**I'm sure our friend Susan was just trying to play a joke on us.**

*Vicky - 9:38pm*

**she's not usually like that**

*Joanne (Group Leader) - 9:38pm*

**I know. Maybe the book was getting the best of her.**

*Ben - 9:39pm*

**whered you find that fucking book anyway**

*Joanne (Group Leader) - 9:40pm*

**I got the set at a used bookstore. They were selling them as a bundle and I thought it looked interesting. Maybe we should do some more research into its history. It might help everyone calm down if we knew where the book came from.**

*Patrick - 9:41pm*

**Don't bother**

*Patrick - 9:42pm*

I just tried looking up the book online. It doesn't exist

*Vicky - 9:43pm*

What do you mean it doesn't exist??

*Patrick - 9:44pm*

I mean **The Presence** by Laura Coven is not on any website anywhere.

*Grace - 9:45pm*

He's right. I can't find it either

*Ben - 9:45pm*

wait arent books supposed to have like copyright pages or whatever in the beginning

*Joanne (Group Leader) - 9:46pm*

Yes. What about it?

*Ben - 9:46pm*

i have my book open and i cant find one

*Patrick - 9:47pm*

he's right. it's just a blank page

*Patrick - 9:47pm*

**what the FUCK is this book**

*Joanne (Group Leader) - 9:48pm*

**I**

*Joanne (Group Leader) - 9:48pm*

**I don't knowwwwww**

*Grace - 9:49pm*

**Joanne r u okay?**

*Joanne (Group Leader) - 9:49pm*

**I'm fine**

*Joanne (Group Leader) - 9:49pm*

**How about we all log off for today? We can come back to the book later.**

*Vicky - 9:50pm*

**I'm not reading any more**

*Joanne (Group Leader) - 9:50pm*

**We can discuss it later.**

*Patrick - 9:51pm*
**whatever i'm fucking out**

*[Patrick has left - 9:51pm]*

*Vicky - 9:51pm*
**goodnight I guess**

*[Vicky has left - 9:51pm]*

*[Grace has left - 9:51pm]*

*Joanne (Group Leader) - 9:51pm*
**wait**

*[Ben has left - 9:51pm]*

*Joanne (Group Leader) - 9:52pm*
**don't leave me**

*[Joanne has left - 11:59pm]*

*The woman refused to go outside. She barricaded herself indoors, forbidding anything foreign from entering her home before she was absolutely certain it was clean. Some people thought she was over-reacting. Even so, she couldn't stop herself from imagining all of the possible germs and viruses crawling over every surface, ready to infect her at any moment. Her life had become a war against an invisible enemy.*

*The woman feared the unseen.*

# 4.

# CHILDREN OF SHADOWS

"They say they don't know where they came from. It's like they just appeared out of thin air."

"That's ridiculous." Liam rolled his eyes, shifting the backpack strap on his shoulder to a more comfortable position. "They had to have come from somewhere. Someone probably just ... forgot."

"How do you forget painting creepy shadow-children on the walls of an elementary school?" Although the sun was setting, there was still enough light to see Veronica's breath waft in front of her face as she spoke. "Some administrative person probably thought it would be a great idea and no one bothered to tell them otherwise. They're always trying to get weird stuff passed in the school district."

"This is gonna be so scary," Kate whispered to Bryan. "You better protect me from any ghosts we see."

Bryan wrapped an arm around his girlfriend, planting a kiss on her forehead. "I'll protect you from anything, baby girl."

Liam stuck a finger in his mouth. "Barf."

Even though she sneered back at Liam, I could tell Kate was secretly basking in the attention. "You're just jealous," she sniped in reply.

Veronica scoffed. "And you two are disgusting."

As Veronica and Liam made kissing sounds and laughed, I glanced around in an attempt to figure out exactly where we were. I had never actually seen Bloody Elementary in person, only heard the rumors. Its real name was Sunny Elementary, but the town had nicknamed it something a little more sinister once the rumors started circulating. I knew the stories the same as everyone else in our town did, but they always got especially popular around Halloween. And it was because of those stories that we were walking down a dimly lit road as 10 pm approached.

No one knew exactly where they came from; we just knew they weren't in the original plans for the school. They started appearing over the years and now they had gained a sort of legendary status in the area.

The shadow-children.

They were of varying shapes and sizes, all roughly the height of a five- or six-year-old. Each was painted in dark black on the cream-colored walls. There was never an explanation for why they appeared or how they got there. The administrators of the school blamed it on vandals, but no one was ever prosecuted. Because unfortunately, they had worse things to focus their attention on than creepy silhouettes.

Right around the same time the shadows started appearing, students who attended the school started going missing. It didn't happen all at once; spread out over a period of fifteen years or so, there were twelve disappearances. And those were just the ones that were confirmed. There were some families that went completely off the radar without warning. One day they were there to drop their kid off at school and then they were never seen again. Other parents claimed they saw an alarming pattern and completely left town. Sometimes it was difficult to tell who went missing and who had just switched school districts.

Regardless, the missing-person cases had a severe effect

on those that remained. There were no leads, no suspects. It tore the community apart: Everyone questioned each other and people were scared to let their kids go outside alone or after dark. Even worse, the students of Sunny Elementary claimed that the more kids that disappeared, the more paintings appeared inside the school. And every time the school tried to remove or paint over them, they were repainted. The school administration insisted it was teenagers, breaking in and trying to create an urban legend. The police department ended up sending out notifications to the neighboring towns, demanding that whoever was painting them stop or face criminal prosecution. But the kids kept vanishing, the shadows grew in number, and there were never any leads. Eventually, Sunny Elementary was forced to close and the building was abandoned. The shadow-children were supposedly still there, though no one had been in the building for several years. It was a common joke in the area to get dared to spend a night inside or break in at midnight, but no one had ever been stupid enough to do it. That is, until one group two years ago.

Legend had it that four teenagers broke into the school at midnight, inspired by a few too many episodes of "Ghost Hunters." Their goal was to walk around for a bit, document what they saw and then go home. Nothing too nefarious, just to have a little fun and gain some bragging rights. But no one made it out that night. They all just — vanished. For a week or two, there was a rumor going around that one of the teens actually survived. That was never confirmed as no one knew exactly who had even gone in, so there was no way of knowing who did or didn't come out. Regardless, from that night on, it was assumed that anyone who stepped foot in that school, student or otherwise, would never return.

So when my friend group decided they wanted to do something scary in town for Friday the 13th, it was pretty easy to select the location: It had to be the school. Personally, I would've been much more comfortable going to one of the countless haunted attractions that were open in town for the month of October, but everyone else (Liam especially) pushed for a more authentic horror experience. People had been talking about staying the night in Bloody for months, but to our knowledge, no one had actually followed through with it after the incident two years ago.

The only way I agreed to this crazy idea was by insisting we bring tools to arm ourselves with. It made me a little more comfortable to know at least Kate and I had pepper spray. Supposedly, Bryan brought his trusty pocket knife, but I'd never seen him use it for anything other than cutting open boxes. I hoped it would be enough if we had to fend off anyone we met with malintent. If I was honest with myself, though, I really had no idea what I was getting myself into.

"Franny, you good?"

I jumped when Liam's voice broke through my swirling apprehensions, having failed to notice him fall back to walk beside me. I mumbled back, "I'm fine. Although I'm less fine since you used that stupid nickname."

"Ah, c'mon," Liam chuckled, lightly punching my arm. "It's not that bad. Franny's cute."

"It makes me sound like a grandma."

Without turning around, Kate raised her hand in agreement. "Seconded."

"Whatever, *Francesca*, but you better not be thinking about chickening out. We promised we'd do this together. Imagine all the bragging we'll be able to do in school on Monday."

I nodded my head as enthusiastically as possible, which even I could tell wasn't very convincing. "Don't worry, I'm not going anywhere. It's not like I have anything better to do tonight."

Kate blew out a laugh, an edge behind it that I didn't miss. "You never have anything 'better' to do."

Veronica frowned. "What the hell, Kate? Don't be a dumbass."

Shrugging, Kate replied, "Well, she doesn't."

"At least she doesn't waste her time dating an asshole."

"At least she doesn't waste her time pining after what she *lost*."

"I'm not jealous of you."

"Yeah, right. Bitch."

Veronica made a move toward Kate, but Bryan caught her arm. "Ladies, ladies," he interjected smoothly. "Let's try to go at least 10 minutes without trying to scratch each other's eyes out? Please?"

After a moment, Veronica nodded and Bryan released his grip on her upper arm. As he moved ahead to walk with Liam, I caught one last comment that Kate hissed in Veronica's direction, "Don't think I didn't notice that mark on your neck. Whoever you're with now is probably dating you out of sympathy."

Veronica's hand leapt to her neck as her face darkened. She

whipped her head toward Kate like she was about to say something. But instead, she sent her a dirty look before speeding up her pace to walk beside Liam again. Kate just sneered at her from behind before pulling out her phone and starting to scroll through Instagram.

Although the tension between Kate and Veronica had been slowly building over the last few months, it was especially bad recently. Veronica had only dated Bryan for about a month before they broke up, but she never seemed to get over it. She would complain behind his back about every girl he dated after that, which only intensified when he started dating someone else from our own friend group. In the last few weeks, she had expanded her barrage to saying things directly to Kate, instead of just privately. Bryan didn't really do anything about the conflict, and if I was being honest, I was pretty sure it was because he liked being fought over. Not that it was my place to judge those sorts of things.

I was torn from my thoughts when I heard Liam call, "We're here."

By now, the sun had fully set and it was nearly impossible to see more than a few feet in front of us. The streetlights kept the worst of the darkness at bay, but there were still patches of pure black where I could barely make out the shapes of the trees and bushes around us. However, even the black of night couldn't conceal the building looming before us. Although nothing immediately stood out about it, there was a certain heaviness to the air we couldn't ignore. We all felt it as we approached. It weighed down our shoulders, stifled our breaths. Veronica and Liam's chatter slowly diminished to silence when, as if in a trance, we all stopped to stare.

The building was only one floor, stretching out in either direction along the street. The road we were walking on ended in a cul-de-sac right in front of the entrance. The layout of the pavement made me slightly claustrophobic. There were windows on either side of the doors, but they yielded about as much sight as staring into two black holes would. On the rightmost side of the school was a small playground with a slide and play set. A single swing carved a half-smile into the air as it swung in the breeze. It looked like something directly out of one of the cheesy horror movies on Netflix that I always laughed at. But now that I was staring at a desolate playground with a swing moving on its own ... I wasn't laughing anymore.

"Ho-lee shit," Bryan breathed, drawing out each syllable. "This place is wild."

"Do you think all elementary schools look this creepy at night?" I asked softly.

"No way." Kate tried to keep her voice steady and confident, but it still wavered slightly as she spoke. "This one is definitely worse than most."

We all stood in silence for at least a minute, feeling the waves of unease wash over us. I could tell we were all waiting for someone to make the first move, but no one was willing to take the leap. Unsurprisingly, it was Liam who eventually stepped forward.

"Well, we're here till sunrise. Then we can brag to everyone how we spent the night in Bloody and lived to tell the tale. Y'all still in?" The rest of us exchanged looks before nodding, my head bobbing considerably less enthusiastically than the others. "All right. Let's do this." Liam turned to Kate. "You got your tools?"

Kate nodded and stepped forward, Bryan following close behind.

"Wait," I cut in, and they all turned to look at me. "What about security cameras? Won't they be able to see us?"

"Those were destroyed years ago," Veronica replied easily. "We're totally fine."

I still didn't like the idea of opening a locked door in clear view of the street, but I didn't say anything else as the pair approached the door. Apparently, they had done some research into lock-picking to prepare for the night by watching some YouTube videos. To be honest, I didn't have much faith in what they found online, but they seemed confident enough. When Bryan reached the door, he held out a hand. "Let me do it." His words were soft, but loud enough for me to make out from a few feet away.

Kate looked at him, gaze hardening. "I told you I wanted to do it."

"I know, it's just ... I don't want you to get in trouble."

"If we get caught, it's not going to matter who opened the door." She began to reach out for the doorknob, but Bryan placed a firm hand on it. There was a moment of tension between them as Kate's gaze flicked from the doorknob to her boyfriend. After a few seconds, she slowly lifted her hand and held it out. Bryan offered the pick without a word and Kate stepped to the side, eyes focused downward. I glanced toward Veronica and Liam, wondering if they had picked up on the interaction that just occurred, but they were both absorbed in the glow of their cellphones.

A few seconds later, there was a muffled click and the door

swung open. A mischievous grin spreading across his face, Bryan stepped inside and opened his arms wide. "Welcome," he announced, "to the scariest night of our lives."

---

If we thought the outside of the building was creepy, it was nothing compared to the inside. Fall weather had chilled the air to what felt like below freezing and we all blew on our hands to conserve as much warmth as possible. Kate took the opportunity to snuggle up extra close to Bryan, already seeming to have forgotten the interaction that took place seconds prior.

The first area we walked into seemed like a foyer. There was a counter to our right with a glass window in front of it for what I assumed was a receptionist. The glass must've been clear at one point, but now there was a thick layer of dust coating it that gave it a milky, off-white color. Directly in front of us was a wall with two long hallways stretching to our left and right. The school itself couldn't have been more than a block in length, but because of the lack of light, the ends of the hallways seemed to fade to black instead of coming to a distinct end. The sight of these long-abandoned places alone was enough to raise the hair on the back of my neck.

But then, we began to see them. And that's when I really started to feel like we had made a grave mistake.

They were both exactly and nothing like I imagined them. Right near the front door were a girl and a boy standing side by side, holding hands. Facing toward the right side of the hall was a small girl who seemed to be mid-stride, running toward the other end of the school. Going the other direction was a group of three that seemed to be playing a game of "rock, paper, scissors." There were a few others farther down the hall I could just barely make out, but it was difficult to tell what position they were in from this distance. Although the actions of the children seemed innocent enough, something about not being able to see their faces made them feel sinister.

A shiver that had nothing to do with the cold traced its way down my spine. "Are you sure we're not going to get caught?" I asked Kate, clutching the straps of my backpack with both hands.

Kate couldn't quite conceal the glimmer of fear in her eyes when she turned to me. "No way," she said with a confidence we both knew wasn't real. "The police don't think anyone comes here anymore. And besides, there aren't any houses nearby to notice us."

I nodded, still not convinced, but not quite scared enough to leave. It's amazing how much the desire to impress your friends can overpower even the strongest gut feeling that what you're doing is completely wrong.

Pulling his bag off his shoulder, Liam dropped it to the ground and wrestled inside for a moment. I heard a click and the room was suddenly bathed in soft yellow. "Flashlights out, everyone. We gotta find a place to settle for the night."

We all rifled in our respective bags until five distinct beams cut through the darkness. The muted lights illuminated small particles of dust and debris bobbing lightly in the air. It reminded me of the Upside Down from *Stranger Things*. I tried not to think too hard about what sorts of things we might be dragging into our lungs with every breath.

Running my light over the shadow girl on my right, I tried to convince myself that she didn't look as scary with the lights on. I could just make out the grains in the paint on the concrete stone wall, the slight blur of her outline. Even so, as soon as I took the light off her, the unease returned. Kate moved to stand beside me and took a picture of the painting with her cellphone. "For proof," she explained to my concerned look. "No one will believe us otherwise."

"Right or left?" Bryan asked, waving his flashlight down one hallway, then the other. As he did, he revealed several more children painted on the walls, each one mid-movement. When the light moved across them, I could almost imagine that I saw them shift ever so slightly. But it was probably just a trick of the light.

"Right," answered Veronica confidently.

"All right. Here we go."

With Kate and Bryan leading, we began to make our way deeper into the building. The farther we got down the hall, the more I realized that the children weren't the only things decorating the walls. There were also drawings and art projects tacked onto small cork boards and some writing assignments about "My Favorite Toy" and "What I Learned This Year." Although the pieces were colorful and full of smiley faces, the elongated shadows cast by our lights stretched the expressions and made the drawings seem depressing. I tried not to stare at the shadow-children that I passed, but sometimes I couldn't help it. There was something about them that made it nearly impossible to look away. One that was particularly unnerving depicted a little girl with a long pigtail. She was leaning over with both hands cupped around her mouth like she was whispering in someone's ear. What made it weird was the fact that there was no one there for her to whisper to. It took effort to drag my eyes away from it. After that, I tried to keep my gaze forward as much as possible, focused on the two figures of my friends in front of me. Every so often, I would see a flash of light and assumed that Kate had taken another photo.

After we made several turns and I had lost all sense of direction in the darkened halls, Bryan finally paused in front of a door. "This spot looks good," he remarked, waving his flashlight into the room. His light caught on the nametag hanging above the doorframe and I was just able to read "Nap Room" before it was overtaken by shadows again.

As we stepped inside and started to look around, I heard Kate gasp, "Oh my God."

When we all turned to look where her flashlight was pointed, it didn't take long to see what had startled her. There were shadow-children in this room too, but this time, they weren't standing up. The artist probably intended to make them look like they were sleeping, curled up against the walls and underneath the chalk boards.

But in the half-light, they just looked like limp, lifeless bodies.

"They're supposed to be sleeping," Liam said quickly. "I'm sure they didn't mean to make them look ..." He trailed off, not quite able to get the final word out.

"Do we have to stay in this room?" Kate whispered to

Bryan. Her eyes still hadn't left the children painted on the wall.

Her boyfriend paused for a moment, thinking, then gestured to the carpeted floor. "The tile gets super cold at night. This is really the only place we'll be able to sleep comfortably."

There was a moment of silence before Kate grudgingly replied, "Fine. Let's unpack."

The next few minutes were filled with the rustling of bags and the hushed whispers of our group laying out where we were going to attempt to sleep for the night. We positioned ourselves around the best source of light, a small electric lantern that Liam had brought from his camping equipment. It gave off a fluorescent glow that was harsher than the muted beams of our flashlights and we quickly settled around it. As the night wore on, our words began to come more smoothly and flow more freely. We slowly began to forget where we were and once Bryan pulled out Cards Against Humanity and two six-packs of Red Bull, it felt more like a normal sleepover than a dare to stay in the scariest building in town.

"Oh no, you did *not*!" Veronica exclaimed at a particularly gross set of cards while the rest of us screamed with laughter. "That is *disgusting*. I did not ever need to picture Pac-Man like that. I'm scarred for life."

"V, have you never played this game before?" I asked when I was able to breathe again.

"No, but you told me it was like Apples to Apples!" She pointed accusingly at the card in question. "That is *not* in the Apples to Apples I remember."

"Don't be such a baby," Kate laughed.

"Don't be such a bitch."

The mirth faded after that and Liam was quick to pull the next subject card. Before we knew it, it was already midnight. Confidence and caffeine were high, and everyone was excited to conquer the night.

"Only six hours to go!" cheered Bryan as we celebrated the turn of the new day.

"This is easy," I laughed, popping the tab on another energy drink. "Nothing has happened."

Liam rapped his knuckles on the floor. "Don't jinx it!"

A few hours later, once the conversation had slowed to a crawl and people started to yawn, we decided to call it quits and grab some shut-eye before the alarm we set for sunrise rang and we could finally go home.

Maybe I did jinx it. Maybe I was naive. Or maybe they were just waiting. But either way, I woke up some time later to a sound.

When I first opened my eyes, I could make out patterns of light and dark, but not what was causing them. It took a few seconds for my eyes to adjust and my brain to make sense of what I was looking at. I couldn't figure out what had woken me: Everyone else was sleeping and, from what I could tell, the room was quiet and still.

That's when I heard it again.

It was faint, so faint I might've thought I had imagined it, had I not been where I was.

I heard whispers.

I couldn't quite make out what they were saying, but they were definitely voices. They sounded light and airy, like they were echoing from miles away. I sat up, looking around for the source, but the echoes made it impossible to tell where it was coming from. I waited to see if it would stop. But it didn't.

"Guys?" I whispered, glancing across the sprawled figures of my friends. "Do you hear that?" My eyes landed on the last sleeping bag and I froze.

It was empty.

I quickly counted heads, making sure I hadn't somehow missed someone. But no, we were definitely one short. And judging by the faces and hair that I could make out in the dim light ... it was Veronica.

"Veronica?" I slowly slipped out of my sleeping bag and stood up, glancing around the room and shivering as the cold night air touched my skin. "Where are you?" She was nowhere in sight. The rest of the group somehow remained asleep in spite of my frantic whispers. Even the paintings on the walls were still in their slumber. As soon as I spoke, the voices stopped too, leaving the room in a tense silence. *Why would they stop so suddenly?*

Even as my heart began to race, I tried to convince myself that everything was fine. She was probably just stretching her legs or something. She would be back soon.

I was about to sit back down and try to get back to sleep when —

*"Come to us ..."*

It was barely more than a breath, but I knew what I heard. And I knew it had come from the gaping doorway that led to the darkened hallway.

I faced the door. "Veronica," I hissed. "This isn't funny. Get back in here." Although I wasn't completely sure it was Veronica whispering, she was the only other person that was up right now. Who else could it be?

I squinted at the door but couldn't make out anything more than black. A moment later, I heard a soft giggle and the distinct pattering of feet echoing down the hall.

Although my mind was still fogged from sleep, I was pretty sure it had to be Veronica fooling around. She'd pulled some pranks like this before, so it didn't seem too out of character for her. I considered letting her have her fun and going back to sleep, but I didn't like the idea of her running around an abandoned school by herself. I heaved a sigh, muttering a curse under my breath as I gathered up my flashlight (and pepper spray, just to be safe) and shoved on my sneakers. "V, I swear to God you better knock it off. You're not funny." Somehow, I made it to the door without accidentally stepping on any stray hands or feet. They must've been pretty sound asleep, which I found odd, considering the amount of caffeinated beverages they had consumed not much earlier. Once I made it to the hallway, I swept my flashlight down in both directions, searching for that familiar head of dark, wavy hair. But there was no one in sight.

After thinking back on which way we had walked to get to the room, I started down the hall with tentative but steady steps. "I'm serious," I hissed into the darkness. "You're scaring me." Hoping that I would hear some sort of reply, I paused to listen. Nothing. For a moment, I thought I heard another wisp of laughter, but it was so brief it could've easily been the echo of a fire truck or an animal from outside.

Still hoping that this was Veronica playing some sort of prank, I moved down the hall quicker, sweeping the beam of my flashlight side to side and peeking into any classrooms I passed. All I found was more empty space.

Even though I was carefully checking each room I passed, I still almost missed her. It wasn't until I heard a small giggle and a hiss of unintelligible words that I stopped and nearly jumped out of my skin.

"Veronica," I sighed in relief, clutching at my frantically beating heart. "What are you doing here? Why are you sitting on the ground?"

"Shhh." Veronica put a finger to her lips and my questions faded to silence. We stayed there for a moment, her on the ground and me looking over her, before she asked, "Can you hear them?"

"You mean the voices?" I looked back down the hall, then to her. "Yeah. Do you think someone else is in the school? At first I thought it was you whispering, but I guess not."

She didn't respond, instead ushering me toward her. After a moment of hesitation, I obliged and moved to kneel beside her. "What are you doing?" I asked again, turning my hands into fists to stop their trembling.

A smile played across her lips as her eyes gently closed. I stared at her for a few seconds longer. That's when my eyes caught something above her that made my blood run cold.

She was sitting next to the painting of the shadow-child

whispering. And the way she was positioned, it looked like the child was speaking directly into her ear. Her eyes were closed, like she was deep in thought. "Oh shit," I breathed, then waved a hand in front of Veronica's face. She didn't respond. "V, what the hell is going on?"

Veronica sat there for a moment, a dazed expression on her face. Then her eyes opened and locked on mine. "She has something to say to you," she murmured. I tried to stand on weak knees, but Veronica's hand shot out and grabbed my wrist.

"What the fuck?" I tugged, but her grip was like steel. "Let me go!"

Though her fingernails bit into my wrist with a force I didn't know she possessed, her voice was perfectly clear and calm as she repeated, "She has something to say to you. Come. Sit."

"Veronica, stop it! You're scaring me!"

Her eyes flashed. "You have nothing to be scared of. Now sit and listen."

Every muscle in my body screamed at me to run away, but something about her words —

Made me freeze.

Made me turn.

Made me sit.

Made me close my eyes and listen to the shadow on the wall. It felt like I wasn't in control of my body anymore. Something else had taken over and I had no choice but to obey.

And there was nothing I could do to stop it.

I heard Veronica stand and take a few steps away. Her voice was barely a whisper. "Listen."

Part of me still clung to the hope that she would snap out of whatever was wrong with her and tell me it was all a joke. But as the seconds wore on, that hope dwindled down to nothing. She wasn't joking around. She was serious. Just when I was ready to give up and open my eyes, I heard it.

*"Francesca ..."*

The blood froze in my veins. I barely felt myself leap to my feet. I spun around, staring at the wall. "Oh shit," I whispered, the words shaking as they passed my lips.

The shadow-girl that used to be leaning over was standing up, arms hanging at her sides. And even though her eyes were veiled in darkness, I could feel her looking directly at me.

"Veronica," I hissed as I spun back around. "What —" My words dissipated as my mouth went dry.

Veronica was gone.

When I turned back to face the wall, I saw the girl had changed positions again. This time, she was pointing to the left, down the other end of the hallway. I stared at it for a moment, weighing my options.

"Fuck no," I spat at the girl, running to the right. My heart was in my throat, pounding with every step as I raced down the hall. It wasn't until I became completely enveloped in the darkness that I realized I had left my flashlight and pepper spray on the floor when I sat down. But I couldn't go back; my feet wouldn't let me stop running. So I relied on muscle memory and desperate prayer to make it back to the room.

Although it couldn't have been more than a few minutes, it

seemed like hours later when I finally made it into view of the Nap Room. The door was still open and I stumbled inside, my breathing alone loud enough to wake the other members of our party.

Bryan groaned, rolling over to face me. He sat up on his elbows and squinted at me. "Franny? Is it six already?"

"Something's wrong with Veronica," I gasped. I crossed my arms in front of me, desperate to rid myself of the chill seeping into my bones. "I couldn't find her and I heard voices so I walked into the hallway and she was sitting in front of one of the shadow-children and she made me sit where she was and the girl whispered my name and when I opened my eyes she was gone and I think this place is —"

"Wait-wait-wait ..." Kate's bleary eyes met mine and I could see her struggling to process the sudden flurry of words. "Why was Veronica in the hallway?"

"I don't know but I woke up and she was gone and I heard the shadows whispering and —"

Liam had finally gained his bearings enough to put up a hand in my direction. "Francesca, you need to slow down. I can't even understand what you're saying. Did you say the shadows were *whispering*?"

Although I myself wasn't even sure if what I had seen was real, I couldn't stop the words from tumbling forth. "The paintings on the walls ... I saw them move."

Bryan's gaze narrowed. "What do you mean?"

"You remember the painting of the girl that had her hands cupped around her mouth? The one that looked like she was whispering or something? After I heard a voice in my ear, I looked back at her and she was standing up and pointing."

"Are you sure you weren't dreaming?"

"Yes, one hundred percent. I know what I saw. The girl *moved* on the wall."

Liam glanced around the room. "Well, I don't hear any whispers now. And the kids in this room don't seem to be moving. They're just standing there."

"I don't —" I broke off, my mind catching up a second later as the words processed. "What do you mean, standing? They were lying down before."

Liam froze. The four of us turned as one to face the walls. I felt my knees go weak beneath me when I saw them.

Every single child painted on the walls was standing, their blank faces staring straight at the center of the room.

They were looking directly at us.

"What the fuck is going on?" I heard Kate whisper —

— right before the room was plunged into darkness.

I gasped, instinctively putting out my hands to find my friends. There were a few hushed cries, some muffled profanities, before the light came back a second later. When I regained my sight, I could see that my hands had found Kate and Liam. We all looked at each other with wide eyes for a moment. Then we turned to face the walls again.

The children were all pointing now, their tiny fingers aimed toward the door.

"Fucking hell," breathed Bryan. I could feel him shaking beneath my grasp. "They can't — that's not —"

Kate suddenly pulled away. She dropped to the floor, grabbing the lantern in one arm and her backpack in the other. "We're leaving," she hissed as she slung it over her shoulder. "We're leaving *now*."

"No." The harshness of Bryan's tone stopped her in her tracks. "No. We're not leaving without Veronica."

"This place is fucking *haunted,* Bryan! I'm not staying here another second. Besides, she's probably outside already —"

I saw Bryan's hands tense at his sides. His next words were through gritted teeth. "She's our friend, Kate. I'm not leaving until we know she's safe."

Kate gave him a long look. I thought I could see tears building in her eyes. "You never loved me, did you? It was always her."

"What?" Bryan asked sharply, then rolled his eyes. "That's not what this is about."

"You're not even denying it." Kate shook her head as she stepped toward the door. "You always had feelings for her. I knew you never got over her. And now you're choosing her over me." She stopped in the doorframe, turning back to look at Bryan. "If you're willing to kill yourself over her, fine. But I'm sure as hell not going to." And with that, she strode around the corner, taking our best source of light with her.

Bryan spat in her direction. "That bitch," he muttered under his breath before turning to me. "Are you gonna fucking leave, too?"

I shook my head quickly. "No. Veronica is my friend."

Liam quickly nodded. "Not gonna lie, bro, I'm scared

shitless. But I'm not gonna leave you two here alone."

After a moment, I saw Bryan's face soften. "Okay, thanks guys. I'm sorry you had to see ... all that."

"It's okay," I responded quickly.

Bryan nodded; his eyes swept over the children standing around us, still pointing toward the door. "We've gotta find her and get out of here. I don't know what the fuck is up with these kids, but I'm not staying long enough to find out."

We hurriedly gathered up as many supplies as we could, leaving Kate's stuff in the middle of the room. There was no way we were dragging her stuff with us. I figured she could come back herself and get it later. There was no way we were sticking our necks out for her any more than we needed to. Within seconds, we were out the door and standing in the hallway. Even though we only had the weak light of our flashlights keeping the darkness at bay, it somehow felt less claustrophobic than standing in the center of the room, surrounded by those faceless shadows.

"Francesca, where did you see Veronica last?" Bryan whispered to me.

I pointed in the direction I had come from a few minutes earlier. "She was by the painting of the girl whispering on the wall, close to the front door."

"And you didn't see which direction she went in?"

"No. I closed my eyes and when I opened them she was gone."

Bryan pushed back his shoulders, a bit of courage forcing

its way into his voice. "Okay. Let's start retracing our steps and see where that gets us."

We took off down the hall, the pounding of our footsteps like a heartbeat echoing through the halls. We kept our eyes focused ahead and away from the walls. After a few minutes, I paused and looked to the left, searching for the familiar silhouette. But there was nothing there. The wall was blank, completely empty save the chipped coating of tan paint. "It should be here."

Liam's flashlight swept left and right on the wall. "What do you mean?"

"The whispering girl. She's gone." I scanned the rest of the wall. "I swear it was right here!"

"Are you sure?" Bryan asked.

"Yes, I'm sure! The front door is right around the corner. I swear I'm not crazy, she was just —" I looked up to find Bryan looking back down the hall the way we came. When his eyes narrowed, I asked, "What is it?"

"They're all gone," he said softly. "The shadow-children. We didn't pass any when we walked back here."

"What?" I got to my feet, aimed my own flashlight down the hall. He was right. Where all the paintings had been was nothing but plain color. My beam of light shook slightly as I aimed it back toward where I had seen the whispering girl. "Well ..." I began in what was barely a whisper, "where the hell are they?"

Almost as if it was responding to my question, I suddenly heard a hushed echo bounce toward us through the darkness. Judging by the way Liam and Bryan's heads swiveled to the right as well,

I could tell they heard it too. Just like before, I couldn't make out words. It was just a continuous meld of voices, floating through the air.

It came from the same direction the shadow girl had been pointing.

The three of us stole glances at each other. My mind screamed at me to run. It told me to sprint through the front door and never come back. But just like before, I felt like I wasn't in control of my body anymore. There was something overriding the desperate flight instinct flooding my thoughts and senses. I was pretty sure Liam and Bryan felt the same because, as if we all shared the same thought, we began walking toward the sound. It increased in volume with each step we took, growing in intensity. After ten or so strides, I saw the front door appear on our left. As we walked by the front desk, I checked to see if the paintings that had been there when we first walked in were gone too, and they were. It was strange — without the shadow-children leering at every corner, I could almost pretend like I was in a normal school. Almost.

I could tell our flashlight batteries were dying. Their beams were growing weaker, only breaking through a yard or so of the black in front of us before surrendering to the darkness. The voices continued to grow louder, almost completely drowning out my own thoughts.

"We have to be getting close to the end of the hallway!" I shouted after what seemed like endless walking. Bryan and Liam nodded their heads in agreement, but didn't comment further. They were wincing slightly against the intensity of the sound and I could feel myself doing the same.

Then, finally, an image broke through the black. I nearly gasped in relief when I recognized her familiar dark hair trailing down her back, the battered Converses on her feet —

"Veronica!" Bryan yelled, immediately breaking off from our group and racing toward her. "Where have you been? We've —" He broke off, skidding to a halt a few feet behind where she was standing. Her back was to us as she faced the end of the hallway, a plain wall without a door on it. At first, I thought it wasn't a dead end because it seemed like the darkness continued onward. But as I got closer, I realized that the wall was actually painted black instead of tan like the rest of the school. And as I stood there, staring at the dark surface, I started to feel something. I couldn't figure out why, but I felt a sort of — energy in the air. During a storm, when lightning is about to strike, the air tastes sharp in your mouth and the pressure builds behind your eyes and ears. That's what it felt like, except it felt like that energy was condensed into one specific place: the wall in front of us.

"Oh fuck." I could barely hear Bryan's words over the chorus of voices pressing in on all sides. "That's not paint. It's ... *them.*"

That's when I realized: it wasn't black paint on the wall.

It was the shadow-children.

I could see them now, not distinct shapes, but the slight shifts in color roiling in the pale light. They were all piled on top of each other, condensed onto the single surface. Not a sliver of color was visible. The energy radiating off them couldn't be ignored. It felt like there was a black hole drawing me toward the surface. I had to dig my feet into the ground to fight against its pull.

Suddenly, the whispering stopped. It wasn't long before a new voice filled it.

"Isn't it beautiful?" I watched Veronica's eyes look up and down the wall. "All of them in one place. It makes you realize just how small you really are."

"Veronica?" Bryan took a step toward her, but he seemed afraid to get any closer. "What are you doing? What's going on? We need to get out of here."

"No, we don't." Her voice was too sweet, her words too measured. "They're all together now. And so are we."

"Not Kate," Liam cut in. "Kate ran when she heard you were missing."

"She did not run far."

I narrowed my eyes at her words. "What's that supposed to mean?"

With careful movements, Veronica turned her head to look at the wall to our left. We had been so distracted when we first found her that I hadn't even noticed the painting on the wall. It was of a girl, far taller than the other children. She was standing, her arms raised in fists by her head. It took me a moment to recognize the silhouette, but when I did —

"Oh God ..." I stumbled away from the wall, my legs weak beneath me. "That's not ..."

"It is," Veronica answered smoothly. Her head was turned

back to the fully black wall, her expression completely neutral.

In what seemed to be against his better judgment, Bryan stepped forward to place a firm hand on her shoulder. "Veronica, stop fooling around. That's not Kate, that's —"

I watched Veronica's hand shoot out and grab Bryan's wrist. He cried out, but she ignored him. "It's your turn." Her gaze flicked between us. "It's all of your turns."

Bryan tried to tug away, but her grasp was too strong. "Let go of me!" he shouted, his voice hoarse and broken. "V, what are you doing?!"

"I'm doing what must be done."

On her final word, her arm shot forward, throwing Bryan against the black wall. He slammed against the brick and I expected him to stumble back or crumple to the floor.

But he didn't.

He seemed frozen, stuck to the darkness almost like he was glued in place. For a moment, nothing happened and he remained there, pressed against the black. But then the shadows started to move. They seeped over his skin, onto his clothes. Everything they touched darkened and faded into the surface of the wall. I saw his shoulders tense, the back of his neck strain as he tried to pull away, but it was too late. The pulsating shadows were already covering him.

If his face wasn't to the wall and already cloaked in darkness, I knew I would've heard him scream.

I blinked once. Twice. And then he was gone. Absorbed into the black as if he had never been. It happened so fast, I didn't even have time to process what was happening before it was too late.

"Where did he go?" Liam took an unsteady step back, his expression twisted in shock and horror. *"Where the fuck did he go?"*

But I knew where he had gone. And when I looked toward Kate's shadow, there was another standing beside her. Slightly taller, with broader shoulders. It couldn't be, but it was.

I felt a tear roll down my cheek, but my legs couldn't seem to move. I was stuck, frozen, staring at what my friend had become. "Why are you doing this?" I whispered, my voice breaking.

Veronica turned. The smile she gave me did not reach her eyes. "The children who live in these walls get lonely. I made a deal, long ago, to bring them new friends whenever they request it. But this place ... it attracts the darkness in people." She pointed to Kate's darkened silhouette. "She was a selfish coward." Then to where Bryan had stood. "He was obsessive and violent." Her finger moved to Liam. "You treat life like a joke." And finally to me. "And you live life without purpose." She stared at me long and hard before continuing. "I brought you here so you can finally embrace the darkness inside each of you and the children can have what I promised them."

"Fuck you!" Liam screamed at Veronica. "You don't know me!" He stumbled backward and I could tell he was preparing to run. I was doing the same, tensing my legs and steeling my core.

Giving a laugh that made my blood run cold, Veronica answered, "Oh, I know you, Liam, better than you realize. During my time here, the children of shadows showed me the truth. They told me what had to be done. And I will fulfill my promise." She glanced at Kate's figure on the wall. "Unlike some of you, I know who my true friends are."

Before Veronica had even finished what she was saying, Liam sprinted toward the front door. I saw Veronica straighten, put out a hand with her palm facing him. From the wall, a stream of shadows poured forth onto the floor. They slithered across the tile like a snake. From within the swarm, I saw dark hands breaking off and stretching upward before melding back into the entity. Liam was moving fast, but *it* was moving faster. I wanted to cry out to him, to help him — but I was still frozen, watching the horror unfold before me.

I watched it curl up the back of his leg, catching him mid-stride and sending him sprawling across the tile floor. He tried to crawl away, but the shadows dragged him back. First his feet disappeared, then his ankles, then his legs. I couldn't stop myself from wincing at the scream that echoed through the hall and slammed against my eardrums. I squeezed my eyes shut, desperate for it to be over. When I dared to open them again, I saw the shadows retreating back into the wall. I blinked again and saw that there was a third figure next to Kate and Bryan. He stood with his palms open, seemingly pressed against the cinderblock. As horrified as I was, I couldn't look away. The desire to run still sang in my veins, but I felt like doing so would seal my fate. I could feel Veronica's eyes on me as the whispers eventually faded away, leaving me in a silence that was palpable.

I took a deep breath to calm my racing heart. "So I'm next."

Veronica surprised me by replying, "Do you want to be?"

I dragged my eyes away from my friends and back to the

one who used to be. "What?"

"The others were too far from saving. But you ..." She pointed at me delicately, almost in spite of herself. "I think there's still hope for you. If you're willing to accept it. I could give your life the purpose you so desperately crave. I've given the others a purpose on the walls. But you still have a choice to make."

The first glimmer of hope bloomed in my chest and I dared to ask, "What do you mean?" I was still trying to figure out a way to escape, but I wanted to hear what she had to say before I did anything rash.

"When I first met the children, they told me everything about this place. After being locked within these walls for so long, they tend to get bored. There are only so many people to play with, and they need someone on the outside to bring new friends to them. The last time I was here, two years ago, they explained everything."

"Two years?" I realized why that sounded familiar a second later. "Wait ... you mean those kids who went missing?"

Veronica nodded, a sort of proud smile spreading across her face. "The darkest are attracted to this place, but the children could tell that I didn't deserve to live on these walls, just the same way I can tell you don't. They gave me a chance to live if I promised to bring them new friends every so often." She waved her hands around. "And here we are. Now I'm giving you that same opportunity. If you take my place and bring people to them when they ask, then you'll be free."

My mind spun as the pieces connected. "You're the one who escaped, aren't you? The one the police could never find."

She smiled. "I knew you were smarter than you looked."

Although I knew I should've had a much bigger reaction to what I was hearing, I was surprisingly calm. The way Veronica said things so matter-of-factly made me want to listen to her. A part of me realized how horrible it would be, knowing that others would have to be sacrificed so I could live. But now that the shadows were before me, trapped on those cinder block walls, I couldn't bear the thought of joining them.

I looked at her for a long moment. That's when I heard a soft *plunk* come from somewhere behind her, so quiet I almost missed it. My eyes traveled to a droplet of water that had fallen to the floor a few feet behind her, against the wall. I traced its path upward to find that the painting of Kate had a rivulet of water running from where her right eye would be, traveling down to the floor. A tear.

"So," Veronica said knowingly, "what'll it be?"

I looked from her to the three paintings on the walls. I thought about the countless lives that had been lost to this place, the lives I would have to ruin just to save my own.

And I made my choice.

---

"This is *so* creepy!" Pam giggled, clutching her phone in both hands. The beam of light coming from beneath the camera lens lit up the street stretching before her. "I'm scared already and we're not even there yet." As she continued walking, Elizabeth crept up behind her, then jumped to squeeze her shoulders. Pam let out a high-pitched squeal, running forward a few feet before turning around to look at the perpetrator. "Stop it, I'm serious!"

Elizabeth laughed lightly, slowing her pace down to walk with the rest of the group. "You are such a wimp. You're not going to last five minutes. I'm betting either you or Ian will leave first."

"No!" Ian cut in, glaring at Elizabeth and pushing his glasses up the bridge of his nose. "I will *not* be leaving first. Besides, this whole thing was my idea."

Pam looked thoughtful. "Actually, wasn't it Francesca's? She was the one who figured out how to get into the school."

Shaking her head in disbelief, Pam turned to look at me. "Why on Earth do you *want* to stay the night in Bloody Elementary? I'm scared out of my mind just thinking about it."

I shrugged, a smile spreading across my face. "I think once we get inside, we'll get used to it pretty quick. Once you see past the shadows, it's not so scary anymore."

*The boy knew there were monsters beneath his bed. He heard their snarls, felt their coldness chill the room when the sun fell from the sky. The soft glow of his night light did little to dispel their darkness. Every night, when his mother tucked him into bed, he made her lift the bed skirt and look for them. Although she was quick to reassure him, as soon as the door closed and the room was cloaked in black, his terror returned.*

*The boy feared the unknown.*

# 5.

# THE HOUSE ON WINDY DRIVE

"This isn't that weird," Derek muttered again. He glanced at the stack of papers in his hands and shook his head. "Just breathe; this isn't weird at all." Although his feet continued to move him forward, his inner mind rebelled against the words he spoke. This was *extremely* weird. Anyone who knew what had transpired just before this moment was well aware that there was nothing normal about what he was doing.

The newly printed manuscript he held in both hands had started as a joke, a strange series of events that resulted in a stack of papers covered in neat lines of text. Derek had written the fifty-seven thousand word monstrosity in only six days. Even now, looking back, he couldn't quite understand how he had done it. It took a full month and a half to edit it, and another two months to complete the first round of polishing. And that was how the college sophomore ended up holding the draft of a book. From the outside, it seemed like a pretty standard document. The contents of it, though, were anything but ordinary.

Derek had always found the concept of books that were "inspired by dreams" as silly and clichéd. He'd heard it happen to a few writers that eventually had their dream-work published, but the concept itself seemed far-fetched. He rarely remembered his dreams and the ones he was able to recall were usually the stereotypical "falling" dream or "I'm late for something and can't remember what."

But the day before Derek started writing, he did have a dream. And months later, he could still remember every detail.

The dream had begun with Derek standing before a brick house. The structure was aged, but seemed sturdy. His dream-self had an undeniable gut feeling that something terrible had occurred there, but he couldn't picture what. He just *knew*.

Derek blinked once and he was inside the house. Night had fallen, cloaking the halls in blue-black. He could just make out a long staircase to his left that swept up to the second floor. In front of the bottom step, there was an odd discoloration in the wood of the floor. Like someone had scrubbed it with a strong cleaner.

Derek instinctively knew that someone had fallen, had spilled red onto the brown oak. He shivered.

*An accident*, the walls seemed to whisper. *An accident that ended in death.*

Derek blinked again and he was back outside. He turned toward the mailbox and read the address.

10 Windy Drive.

And then he woke up.

At first, he didn't think much of it. He mentioned it as a passing remark to his friend Jason, expecting nothing more than a laugh. But Jason took it seriously.

"That's sick, man," Jason replied, much to Derek's surprise. "Sounds like a scary movie or something. You should write it down and send it to a movie producer. You could get rich."

Derek gave him a look. "That's not how that works."

"Well, I dunno. Maybe write a book about it if the movie deal doesn't pan out."

"You think I could write a book?"

"You'd have better luck than I would. You've gotten a better grade than me on every English assignment this year."

Derek had shrugged and grudgingly agreed, but didn't really give it much more thought. People had weird dreams all the time and they usually forgot about them within a day or two. Even so, as time passed, his mind kept returning to the idea. He tried to shove it aside for more important things, like schoolwork or soccer practice, but it always managed to resurface when he least expected it.

After nearly a week of this, he gave in and opened a new document on his laptop. It was his first time writing something that wasn't assigned for school, but he fell into a rhythm quicker than he expected. He lost himself in the words, the pieces of the story falling into place with what seemed like divine inspiration. One week and many sleepless nights later, Derek had a fully realized manuscript. Well, almost. He couldn't figure out how to end it. The rest of the book seemed to pour endlessly from his fingers. Once he got to a certain part, though, it felt like he hit a brick wall. He decided to try to read it all over again and see if something came to him when he reached the end. While he read over it, he made some edits along the way, just like he had done with the writing he did for school. When he got to the last page, he realized he was no closer to figuring out how to end the story than when he started. So he tried reading it again. And again. And again.

Once it had moved from a barely readable first draft to something more polished, Derek could hardly believe he had put the (mostly) completed book together. The writing didn't even sound like him. Maybe the weirdness of the whole thing was getting to him, but the story felt like it had been written by someone much older and wiser. Worst of all, as he held it in his hands, he couldn't ignore the fact that it was incomplete. It was like an itch he couldn't quite scratch. He lay awake at night for hours, mulling over the story, willing something to come forward. But he never got it to click.

Just when he felt like he was at a complete loss, an idea suddenly sprang to mind. Where had this house come from? He had no idea when he first started writing … but wasn't it true that everything you saw in a dream you had seen at some point in real life? Derek knew it was true for faces — maybe it was true for locations as well. So, just for the hell of it, he decided to plug "10 Windy Drive" into his phone. To his shock, he discovered it was a real place, only a half-mile walk from his home. How his unconscious mind had come up with an address that he couldn't remember ever seeing, he had no idea. It was probably buried somewhere deep in his subconscious. Even so, it felt strange to write a fictional story about a real place he had never even visited.

That's when it hit him. Maybe, just maybe, standing in front of the house would help him find the ending to his story. It could be the burst of inspiration he'd been looking for. And besides, he had nothing else to lose.

And that's what led him to stand alone in front of a decrepit house, a thick stack of papers clutched to his chest. He ran his eyes slowly over it, taking in every detail. The shutters were chipped and faded, closed tight against the windows. The bricks on the outside were clearly weathered with age and the structure itself seemed to carry a presence with it that Derek could feel from the street. In his mind, he hadn't completely believed the house was a real thing. Now that he was standing before it, it was almost overwhelming. He was so lost in thought that he didn't hear the footsteps approaching from behind him.

"Can I help you?"

The deep, gravelly voice caused Derek to jump. He spun around and found his gaze locked with that of a tall, broad-shouldered man. The man's face was half-shadowed with scruff, eyes hollowed and slightly too wide for his face. His scraggly gray hair concealed most of his eyes, but what Derek could see of his glare made it clear that the man wasn't happy to see him outside the house.

"Oh — um ..." Derek stuttered. He hadn't thought of what he would say if anyone saw him. Come to think of it, he hadn't really thought at all about what would happen when he arrived. He just knew he had to see the house in person. "I was just ... looking at the house." Derek's eyes moved to look at the mail in the man's hand. He read the address stamped on the top-most envelope. "You live here?"

The man followed where Derek's gaze was aimed and shifted the rest of the letters so they were concealed from view. "Yes," the man replied slowly. "What about it?"

Unable to think of an alibi fast enough — and unable to stop himself — the truth tumbled forth from Derek's mouth. "Well, um, this is going to sound a little weird. But I ... I wrote a book about your house."

The man raised an eyebrow. "Oh. Why the hell would you

do that? You know my house?"

"No, I ..." Derek struggled to explain. "I was ... inspired, I guess. I had — a dream about it." He turned away as his face began to flush. He needed to stop talking before he let something slip that he would regret. He was quite sure now that this was definitely weird. "You know, I — I'm sorry, I didn't really think this through. I should probably —"

"No," the man replied a little too forcefully. He smiled and Derek could've sworn he saw something darker behind his eyes. "I want to hear about it."

Derek couldn't tell if he was joking or not, but it was too late now to backtrack. "Um ... okay." He hesitantly held out the slightly wrinkled stack of papers, his hands shaking a bit. "Here."

The man took them and began to leaf through them. "*The House on Windy Drive*," he read. "What's it about?"

"Well, it takes place in your house. It starts with this accident. There's a brother and sister who are playing, and the sister accidentally falls down the stairs. She hits her head really hard and ... she dies." It suddenly struck Derek how morbid it all sounded, but he forced himself to continue. Hopefully, the man wasn't easily offended — or disturbed. "Decades later, the brother is haunted by his sister's ghost. Her spirit is still in the house and he needs to find a way to set her free."

For the first time since he started speaking, Derek looked up. The man was staring at him. It might've been a change in light, but he seemed pale.

On instinct, Derek continued, struggling to fill the uncomfortable silence. "The brother's named Michael, and I —"

"William," the man breathed.

Derek started. "What?"

"The brother's name is William." The man stepped toward Derek. "*My* name is William."

Derek's mouth hung open, his mind blank. He jolted when the man moved to grip his shoulder with one hand. Before Derek could protest, he pulled him toward him and lowered his head to whisper in his ear.

"My sister," he murmured, "she wants me dead." The man's fingernails cut into Derek's skin. "It was an accident. I didn't mean it; I was just a child. But maybe your story ... maybe you can help me explain. *Please*, help me." Receiving no reply from the stunned boy, his grip tightened. His next words stole the breath from Derek's lungs.

*"She's coming for me."*

*There is one fear that we all share. Though we may shove it aside and try to push it from our thoughts, it refuses to be silenced. If we truly consider it, even for a moment, the coldness of the unknown seeps in and we feel true helplessness. It is the great equalizer, the thing we are both fascinated and repulsed by. But one day, we will all experience its truth.*

*We all fear the inevitable.*

# 6.

# A Weighted Soul

"That night, my brother left and we never saw him again. They found his body a few weeks later."

The room was quiet, the air still. Even though we didn't know the boy Rachel spoke of, after her witness, I felt like I almost did. The way she described him — I could feel her connection to him, her pain at his passing. I could sense the space where he was missing, felt where he should be, but wasn't.

No, I realized. I wasn't thinking of Rachel's brother. I was sensing where my own brother was missing. I had been feeling it for quite some time, but something about hearing someone else speak of it made it more prominent and biting. Sitting in this room, surrounded by so many others who had gone through similar losses, I couldn't ignore the dull ache in my heart.

"Thank you for your testimony, Rachel. It was very brave," our group leader said. Her voice was perfectly balanced, giving off an air of manufactured empathy. At the start of the meeting, she had said her name was Bethany. "We'll continue to keep Corey in our thoughts and prayers. Would any of the other new faces tonight like to share their story?"

Even though she wasn't going to say it, we all knew there was only one other person at the meeting who hadn't shared anything yet: me. I didn't particularly feel like talking, but when the silence stretched on and it became clear that no one else would step in to fill it, I heaved a sigh and cleared my throat.

"Hi. Um, my name is Cassidy."

"Hi Cassidy," the rest of the group said in unison.

"I — uh ..." My mouth had gone dry. I licked my lips before pushing past the nerves holding back my words. "My brother Cameron died a month ago. He was my twin and ... it was really sudden." I paused, trying to gauge how much I should say. After a moment, I figured there was nothing left to lose. Literally. So I let the words flow. "We're both — I'm a junior in high school. He had a habit of hanging out with the wrong kind of people and he went to a lot of parties. The night it — happened — he was at one, at his friend Jane's house. They were celebrating someone's birthday, I think. I wasn't there, I don't normally get invited to stuff like that. But I heard from a friend later that there was a lot of drinking, some drugs. Nothing too crazy, just having fun.

"Sometime around one, Cameron decided to go home. He and I had just gotten our licenses a few weeks earlier, and he was still kinda learning. The police officer told us that at one point during the drive, he stopped at a red light. He was waiting to turn left at a pretty busy intersection. I don't know why it was so busy that late at night, but it was. And that's when he got rear-ended." There was a light intake of breath from the room and I hurried to explain. "The crash itself wasn't that bad; the problem was my brother — he pre-turned the wheel. And when he got hit, his car moved forward and to the left, toward where it had been turned — right into the path of an oncoming truck." I swallowed, forcing back the tears that welled behind my eyes. I refused to let them fall. I had cried enough this past month. Even so, my throat closed, and I knew I had run out of words.

Bethany nodded like she understood, as if she could possibly know what I was feeling. "Thank you for sharing your story with us,

Cassidy. It was very brave of you." Then she started talking about how important it is to rely on others or something like that. But I wasn't listening. As time passed after I finished speaking, I began to feel more and more ashamed. The rest of the group didn't want to hear all of that. All they needed to know was my brother was dead. Sharing his story hadn't fixed anything or made me feel better. It had just turned his death into a Driver's Ed lesson.

I counted down the minutes until the session ended. Although it was my first time attending, I could already tell it would be my last. I had never been very good at sharing my feelings and I would do just as well writing about it in a journal or something. I might even do better, since after I was done writing, I could burn the pages and no one would get the chance to read them. After the meeting, however, I couldn't exactly un-say what had been said. Every time I thought about the rest of the group's sympathetic glances after I finished speaking, I felt my stomach drop. It just felt so wrong talking about it out loud. Like whenever I repeated the story, it made it more real and solidified the fact that I would never see my brother again.

It was only once I was in the safety of the car that I let myself cry. I kept telling myself that I wouldn't anymore, that it had been a month and I needed to move forward, but I couldn't stop. I felt him everywhere. I missed him *so* damn much. I hadn't even realized how much I loved him until he wasn't there to play pick-up basketball with or help me with a chemistry assignment or even just listen to me vent about how frustrating high school was. It was so natural for me to lean on him for support that I didn't even notice until that support was gone and I went tumbling down.

*If only*, I thought to myself, wiping at the tears that seemed to pour endlessly from the corners of my eyes. *If only I had known. If I had had a chance to say goodbye, to tell him how much he meant to me, things would be different.*

But I hadn't. And they weren't.

---

In the days that followed, nothing really changed. I continued going to school, trying to get back into the normal routine of studying. The weird popularity that surrounded people who awful things happened to had worn off, which was nice. At least I didn't have to deal with the people crying over me at lunch, saying how much they missed my brother when we both knew they had never even been friends. The ones who were really hurting were much more quiet about how they felt. I made a point never to cry at school. Once or twice I had to escape to the bathroom to pull myself together, but I never made a scene. I didn't want any more attention than what was already on me.

Luckily, that wasn't really a problem anymore. I still got a few sad looks from time to time, but I just ignored them. Teachers were still pretty lax about when I turned in assignments and I noticed they were also a tad nicer when grading. Even though I didn't really need it, the extra help was appreciated. School itself was a nice distraction until 2 pm, when I was plunged back into my lonely reality. I found myself taking long walks, people-watching, doing anything that wouldn't remind me of him. But I never forgot, not completely.

On the Wednesday of that week, my plan sort of backfired on me. I was walking along one of the quieter streets near our school, trying to decide which coffee shop I should sit in to work on my calculus homework, when I saw him. He had black hair and dark eyes, with sharp features. He had to be a couple of years older than me, probably early twenties, but he held himself like he was much older. I couldn't quite place where I knew him from. After a second, I had almost convinced myself that my mind was playing tricks on me and I really didn't know him at all. But then our eyes met, and he smiled and waved. I couldn't exactly avoid the interaction now, seeing as we were walking directly toward each other. Taking a breath, I mentally braced myself for a conversation.

"Hi!" he said when we were a few feet away. He motioned me to the side of the sidewalk so we could talk without getting in anyone's way. "Weren't you at the group session the other night?"

"Uh, yeah," I said slowly. That's right, I thought I remembered seeing him there. That must've been why he was familiar.

"Your name is Cassidy, right?"

I nodded, then struggled for a second longer before giving up. "I'm sorry, I can't remember yours."

He shrugged. "Friends call me Lou." He paused for a moment, and when he spoke again, his voice was less conversational and more serious. "Your witness was really powerful. I lost someone close to me a few months ago and it definitely struck a chord."

"Oh." My mind flashed back to that night and how embarrassed I had been immediately after speaking. "Really?"

"Yeah. It was so honest and real. I appreciated how vulnerable you were. You didn't hold anything back."

I could feel my cheeks growing warm from the unexpected praise. "Thank you."

"You're welcome." He sighed and ran a hand through his hair. "I know the first few months are the hardest. Time doesn't exactly heal the wound, but it does make it sting less. If you ever need anything, or just want to talk, let me know and I'd be glad to help."

Even though I barely knew the guy and this whole conversation was a chance meeting, I couldn't help but feel comforted by his words. Here was someone who wasn't just pretending to know what I was going through. He *really* knew, and he cared enough to try to help. "Thanks," I replied, allowing a small grin to spread across my face. "That really means a lot."

He smiled back, then threw a glance toward the people walking around us. "They have no idea how lucky they are," he chuckled darkly. "It feels like our lives have stopped completely, and the biggest thing they have to worry about is what Netflix show they're going to watch next."

I nodded again, feeling his words more than I wanted to admit. I built up the courage to add, "It all just happened so suddenly. I feel like ... if I had even a little warning that it was coming, it wouldn't have hurt so much."

Lou turned to me, a thoughtful expression on his face. "It's not impossible, you know."

I turned to him, sure I had misheard. "What?"

"It's not impossible to know that sort of stuff. You just need to know who to ask." Before I could even begin to process what he had said, he looked down at his watch and sighed. "Well, I gotta get going. Nice talking to you!" He turned away, and just like that, he was gone.

I stood there for a few more seconds, trying to wrap my head around what had just happened. What did he mean, it wasn't impossible? Of course it was, that's what made death so hard to deal with. No one could know the day they died. I must've misunderstood whatever he had said.

But still, as I continued walking in the opposite direction, I couldn't help but feel like I was turning my back on something much bigger than I realized.

A few days later, I was sitting in a Starbucks, drinking a black coffee and trying to force my way through an essay that was due three days earlier. It really wasn't coming together and I rubbed at my tired eyes, willing the caffeine to kick in sooner rather than later.

That's when I heard someone say, "Oh, hey Cassidy!"

I looked up and there was Lou, standing by my table. He gave a small wave with the hand not holding a coffee cup and asked, "How are you?"

My brain took a moment to transition from AP Literature to real-world conversation. "Um — fine," I managed eventually. "How are you?"

He shrugged. "I'm doing fine." His eyes narrowed at me, studying my face. "You look confused. Tough assignment?"

"Yeah," I replied, heaving a sigh. "Just this stupid essay."

"Oh, I remember those days," he chuckled. "Well, I can see you're pretty busy. I guess I'll see you around."

As Lou turned away, something deep inside me protested. I felt like I was losing something, like I was missing out by letting him walk out the door.

"Wait."

I hadn't even realized I had spoken the word aloud until he looked back at me. "Yes?" he asked.

"There's ... something I want to ask you."

He casually walked toward me, almost like he had been expecting me to say something. When he reached my table, he took the seat across from me. Being so close together, I could see the sharpness of his eyes, the high cheekbones that defined his features. "What is it?" he asked when I didn't immediately speak.

"You —" I struggled to put my question into words. "You mentioned something last time I saw you. About — about it not being impossible to know ..."

... *the day you die*. I couldn't finish the sentence, but it felt like the air around us whispered it all the same.

Lou nodded, his expression neutral. "Yes, I did."

"But ..." I shook my head, confused. "That's impossible."

He shrugged. "Only for most people. Lucky for you, I'm not like most people."

Something about his words chilled the air, and I could feel

my heart rate pick up in my chest. "What are you talking about?"

Lou looked straight into my eyes. "I can tell you what you want to know, Cassidy."

He wasn't joking, I could tell. But even though it was impossible for what he was saying to be true, it didn't feel like he was lying, either.

Without reason to, I found myself believing him.

Silence hung between us for a long while. I didn't realize he was waiting for an answer until he asked, "So do you want to know?"

I froze. "You would just tell me?"

"I mean ..." He raised and lowered his hands like weighing a scale. "There's always a price to things like this. But wouldn't it be worth it?"

*A price.* What price was he talking about? But as I stared into his dark eyes, I thought I could see what he meant. I couldn't agree to this, couldn't possibly believe what he was saying. That's when the tiniest voice in the back of my mind whispered, *What if?*

What if what he was saying was true and I could actually know? Wouldn't that make everything clearer? My mind was a blur of questions.

He glanced down at his watch, drummed his fingers on the table. "I don't have all day, Cassidy. Is it a deal or not?"

"A deal?" I asked. "What deal?"

He raised an eyebrow at me, like I already knew.

And I did know.

"Final offer," he said, gathering his coffee in one hand and moving like he was about to stand. I held my breath, bit my lip.

Then —

"Yes. It's a deal."

His lips curled around the word: "Excellent." He held out a hand to me. Slowly, my own hand shaking slightly, I reached out to grab it. I felt a tug and was pulled toward him. We were both leaning across the table, faces inches apart. I squinted my eyes shut as he leaned closer, felt his breath across my cheek. Then, he whispered, *"Wednesday, November 18th, 2020."*

He drew away and I fell back into the seat. My heart sank down into my chest, eyes lowered to the ground. I couldn't meet his gaze. That was so close. I was expecting it to be much farther off, not — eleven years.

"Is something wrong, Cassidy?" I heard Lou say.

"No," I responded quickly, gaze still fixed down. "It's just ... sooner than I expected."

He chuckled. "Well, aren't you glad you know, then?"

I thought for a moment. "I guess so," I said, then looked up.

The booth was empty. I heard the bell at the front of the door toll as the door shut behind him.

---

As soon as he left, it was as if someone pressed "play" on the world. I could hear the hiss of the coffee machines, the gentle chatter of patrons. And there I sat in the middle of it all, the one thing still in the midst of the constant motion.

I felt like I could breathe again, like my lungs were fuller than they had been before. My brain instantly went into denial, trying to convince the rest of me that I had imagined the whole thing. But there was something deep inside that told me it was real. I could feel something darker biting at the back of my mind that insisted this was no dream.

I pulled out my phone, surprised to find my hands were still trembling. I opened the Calendar app and scrolled down to November 18, 2020. He was right, it was a Wednesday. Seeing it there, as a real date, shook me more than I wanted to admit. Even though I wasn't even sure I completely believed him, I felt like I should do something to mark the day. I opened an event, thought about what to write for a moment, then settled on a single question mark. Because who knew what was real anymore?

I took a few moments to gather myself, then reopened my laptop and tried my best to continue the assignment. As the minutes passed, I felt like I was getting lighter and lighter. Like a weight had been lifted off my shoulders. Sure, he could've been lying. But if he was telling the truth, I had a total one-up on things. Because of that, I found myself *wanting* to believe him. I reveled in the feeling that I was in control of something, that I was able to look ahead toward the biggest plot twist of my life.

I felt like I had power over my future.

The rest of the school week felt weird and disjointed. Something had drastically changed in me, but it wasn't something I could just talk to family and friends about. This was my secret, my future that was in my control. This wasn't for anyone else to know or deal with. It had to be me. Besides, even if I told them, would they have believed me?

Would I have believed my brother if he had told me?

As I continued going through the motions, there was one question in particular that kept bugging me at the back of my mind: Now what? Now that I knew this information, this date that would supposedly end my life, what was I supposed to do? I thought a lot about what I could do with eleven years to live — run away to LA, buy a house with a lover, hitchhike across the country — but none of them seemed sustainable for even a few months, let alone over a decade. Eventually, after a few days of thought, I picked quite possibly the most boring option of them all: I would continue living a normal life. But there was a catch.

Those eleven years had to be for me and only me. There wasn't room for anyone else. If I was truly dying in 2020, that wasn't nearly enough time to do all the things I wanted to do when it came to romance. But if I wanted to make the most of the time I had left, I would need to complete my education and at least get some of my bearings so I would have the income to do the things I wanted to. Yes, I would continue on my original path. But if something came up that made me want to abandon it and take a risk, I would.

Because in the end, 2020 wasn't that far off. If things turned sour, at least I knew where the line was drawn.

---

And that's how I left it. For the next several years, I continued living. I graduated high school, got into a decent college, and worked toward a Public Relations major. Every year on November 18th, I would get unnecessarily tense. I couldn't help myself. Even though I knew the date wouldn't be meaningful for several more years, I felt like there was a weight hanging over me on that day. Sometimes my friends would ask me if something was wrong, but I never let the secret slip. That's what made it a secret, after all.

It stayed that way for most of my time in college. And over time, the memory of that fateful day became more and more faded. Although it had never left my mind for more than a moment in high school, there were days which passed in college when I never even thought about it. Sometimes I was able to convince myself that it had never actually happened, that it was some weird hallucination or dream that was so lifelike it had only felt real at the time. But then again, the memory still felt very real on every November 18th that passed. Regardless, I'd be lying if I said there wasn't something liberating about believing in the date. I didn't have to worry about doctor's appointments or major catastrophes. I knew where it would end for me, so I had no need to worry about uncertainties. It was almost freeing, in a sense.

By the beginning of my senior year, I had decided to move to my dream city, Los Angeles, and find some sort of job there after I graduated. I could live out my years there, away from family, without anything holding me back. Sure, it would suck to lose friends, but I could always make new ones. The rest of my family was upset when I told them about my plans, but they eventually accepted it when they saw how excited I was. Although a part of me was sad to leave them behind, I knew that in order to really embrace who I wanted to be, I needed to get as far away from the past as possible.

In high school, when I thought of the future, I was scared and intimidated. Now the years ahead seemed like blank pages of an adventure story. Who knew that one simple piece of knowledge could change someone's life so drastically?

By the midpoint of my second-to-last semester, I was at my peak. Acing my classes, gearing up for graduation, enjoying quirky electives and nights out on the town.

And that's when life proved it wasn't quite done with surprises.

Austin Rodgers was someone I'd heard vaguely about during my years at university, but our paths had never crossed. At least, they never crossed until one night at my favorite bar. Everyone was celebrating midterms being over and the proximity of graduation. Drink flowed freely and our laughter was light and airy. And it was mid-laugh that I saw him.

I'd heard that he was cute, but it was different in person. He wasn't like the guys you see on television, skin too smooth, hair too perfect. He was good-looking in a natural way, which somehow made me fall for him even more. When our gazes caught, he got up, walked over to me and introduced himself. He asked if I would like another drink. I said yes, and he ordered one. We talked the rest of the night, until the bar closed. Then we walked back to his apartment and talked some more. With tipsy minds and hands entwined, we watched the sunrise through his window on the fifth floor. He walked me back to my place and, after kissing me gently on the forehead, wished me goodbye.

Suddenly, my plans of being alone the rest of my life seemed *much* less appealing.

I did end up moving to LA as I had planned, but there was one more person involved in the process. It seemed like the stars were aligning when we both found jobs in the same area of the city by the end of our senior year. We celebrated graduation and headed to California a month later. We loved our jobs, each other, and the new life we planned together. Week by week, I felt myself falling away from my family back home, but I had all I needed to be happy. My parents talked about moving toward us, but I told them I needed space and distance. After my painful high school years, I wanted nothing more than to start fresh. And I was living my dream.

That year, for the first time, November 18th came and went without my noticing.

On the two-year anniversary of our moving to LA, Austin proposed. It was a small affair over a candlelit dinner at the most expensive restaurant we could afford, but it was the most romantic thing I could've imagined. We got married a year later at the beach and moved into a larger apartment together. He literally swept me off my feet and carried me through the doorway like they did in the movies. Everything was perfect.

One year, four months, and twenty-eight days later, I was sitting in front of the television next to my husband. There was a glass of champagne in one hand, the other holding a monitor that showed our daughter sleeping peacefully in the adjacent room. We watched the countdown, then kissed as the ball reached the bottom of the screen. Austin wrapped an arm around me, smiling as animated confetti burst to ring in the new year.

But when four numbers popped on the screen, my smile faded. The ten years of my life flashed by and I was once more confronted with the memory of that day.

"Happy 2020!" cheered the announcer. "Auld Lang Syne" started to play, but I could barely hear it.

My eyes didn't leave the number as I did the math.

I had less than a year to live.

---

The change was immediate. Austin noticed right away. He asked what was wrong, if there was something upsetting me, but I just told him it was post-holiday blues. I went back to work in a haze, barely making it through the motions. Every time I saw a calendar, a clock, or anything that had to do with the seconds slowly ticking down to November 18th, I found I couldn't breathe.

After a particularly difficult moment when Austin asked me about making plans for a Thanksgiving weekend vacation, I couldn't stop myself from collapsing into his arms as tears streamed down my face.

"Cass," he whispered, drawing me close and running a hand through my hair. "Please, honey, tell me what's wrong. I can't help you if you don't talk to me."

I shook my head into his shoulder, clutching him with all the strength I could muster. "I can't," I breathed. I longed to tell him what I knew, but the words wouldn't come. How would I even begin?

That night, I left Austin sleeping in our bed and crept into the other bedroom to where Emma was resting. She had curly black hair like her father, all mussed from sleep, and a tiny smile danced over her lips as she slept.

Staring at our daughter, the tears started falling again and I found myself pressing a hand over my mouth, struggling to stifle the sobs that threatened to ruin her beautiful slumber. I knelt next to her crib, reaching a hand through the bars to caress her cheek. She let out a soft sigh, her small hand reaching up to touch mine.

This could've been avoided, *should've* been avoided. If I had stayed with my original plan, I wouldn't have to cope with leaving my daughter and husband behind. I should've been doing what I always dreamed of: partying in LA, going celebrity-watching, and living a solo life. I thought of where I could be right now, having fun like I always dreamed of, not stricken with the thought of abandoning everything I loved.

But then I thought of all the wonderful things I had experienced. Meeting Austin, getting married, moving in together, the birth of our daughter, Emma babbling and falling asleep in my arms. If I had followed my original, self-absorbed path, I would've never lived through any of those beautiful moments that defined the person I was. And it was that thought that steadied my breathing and steeled my heart.

I realized my family needed me. For the little time I had left, I had to be there for Emma and Austin. I knew when I was going to die. That meant I knew exactly how much time I had left. And I was going to make that time count.

The next morning, I told Austin I wanted to go on a vacation as soon as possible. At first he seemed unsure, but when he asked if it would help me and I said yes, he softened. He was able to convince his boss to let him take off from work, and he, Emma and I went on a week-long trip to the beach. It was wonderful, watching her play in the surf and build in the sand. Austin and I had beautiful mornings, sipping coffee and watching the sunrise. At night, we played soft music and slow-danced in the half-light of dusk just as we had in his college apartment all those years ago.

When I came back, I was a new person. I spent every moment possible with my family. Even if I was exhausted after a day at work, when Austin asked if I wanted to go out to dinner, I immediately agreed. I made the most of every second, drank in the sound of my daughter's laugh and the feel of my husband's kiss. The days passed quickly, but they were full of the things that gave my life meaning and joy.

One morning, I opened my eyes. I sat up in bed, reached for my phone. The screen flashed to life and the date appeared.

November 18th.

---

As much as I tried to keep myself calm, the sight of it made my blood run cold. It was actually here. The day that had been a waking nightmare of mine for the past eleven years of my life was finally here. At the top of the screen was a reminder for an event called "?". I quickly deleted the notification; it wasn't like I was going to forget it any time soon. Once Austin left for work, I called my office and told them I was sick and wouldn't be able to come in. My boss sounded annoyed, but in 24 hours, it wouldn't matter if she was angry with me or not. I needed to spend my last moments with my daughter.

Instead of driving Emma to daycare like I usually did on Wednesdays, I took her downstairs and had breakfast with her. She was extremely grateful for the additional attention and I spent all morning playing with her. I wanted to live every second to the fullest, but I couldn't stop myself from being on edge. Every sound made me flinch, every buzz from my phone caused me to jump. I didn't know what I was waiting for, but I knew it was coming. Perhaps that was the worst part.

But as I sat there, drawing with Emma, something came to mind that I hadn't thought of before. When I died, it was possible that whatever caused my death would be dangerous enough to kill the people around me. And at the moment, my daughter was sitting less than a yard away from me.

I jumped to my feet with a gasp, so suddenly that Emma began to cry. Using my phone to check the time, I realized Austin would be home in less than an hour. As soon as he got home, I needed to get away from them. I needed to protect them from whatever was going to happen to me. That was all I could do now, the last thing I could do for them. I gathered Emma in my arms, shushing her and rocking her until her cries quieted. Then, after one last kiss, I placed her down in the playpen and started making dinner. Such a normal thing to do, considering the circumstances. But it was the only thing to do.

Austin came home right as I was setting the table. He kissed me tenderly, asked about my day, then went to say hello to Emma. I felt numb, living each moment outside of my own body. Nothing seemed real; every motion I made felt like treading water.

After dinner, I decided. After dinner, I would say goodbye.

I listened to Austin talk about his day while we took turns helping Emma with her pieces of puffed cereal. There was a ringing in my ears that almost completely drowned out his words, and I nodded and "Mmhm"ed my way through the meal. It seemed to be over in an instant, and then we were drying the last of the dishes.

A weight settled over my shoulders, and I knew it was time.

Drying my hands with a towel, I turned to my husband. "Austin?"

His bright hazel eyes met mine. "Yeah?"

"I ..." I forced the words past trembling lips. "I'm going out. I need some time to myself."

His brow crinkled, but all he said in reply was, "Okay. I can watch Emma; it's not a problem."

"Thank you," I said, holding the tears back as best I could. Then, after a moment of silence, I wrapped my arms around him. He must've felt something different in the embrace, because he let me hold him without complaint for much longer than we normally did. "I love you, Austin," I whispered. "I love you so, so much."

"I love you, too," he murmured back.

I took in his scent, the sound of his breathing, the feel of his arms around me. I burned them into my mind. And then I pulled away. With all my being, I wanted to kiss him one last time. But I found I couldn't. I knew if I did, I wouldn't be able to make it out the door. As I walked toward the other room, I heard him call, "Text me when you're headed home!" My throat had closed by then and I couldn't reply. Not that there was anything left to say.

Emma was playing with a large-piece puzzle when I saw her. I was sure she had no idea what she was doing, but she was content putting the pieces next to each other and trying to make them connect like she had seen Mommy and Daddy do countless times before. I lowered myself beside her, wrapped my arms around her. Surprised at the sudden contact, she let out a gurgle and played with my hair in her little hands. Running my eyes over every detail of her face and smile, I placed a kiss on her forehead before drawing her close to me.

I held her as long as she would let me before she started to squirm. I reluctantly put her down and watched her wrestle with the pieces again for a moment. Then I stood. I went into my bedroom, withdrawing three envelopes from the drawer in my vanity. I had written them weeks ago: one addressed to Austin, one to Emma and one to the family I had left behind all those years ago. At first, I had tried to make a video for each of them. I thought that if they could see my face, hear my voice, that I could somehow make them understand.

Every time I sat in front of the camera, though, something inside me would break. Tears would flood my eyes and stifle the words I so desperately wanted to say. I could never even start. So I opted for pen and paper.

I placed Austin's envelope under his pillow where hopefully he wouldn't find it until I was long gone. I hid Emma's in her room, behind some of her stuffed animals.

I prayed one day she would understand.

The letters didn't contain the truth. I didn't want Emma to grow up thinking her mom was crazy — or that I had taken my own life. What the letters did contain was *my* truth: how much I loved them and would miss them. I tried to make it as clear as possible that although I couldn't stop what was coming, it wasn't my choice. The letter to my parents was more of an apology, telling them that I was happy and had lived a good life, but I was sorry I hadn't made them a larger part of it. I shoved their letter into the mailbox before walking toward the car parked in the street.

I barely made it to the driver's seat before I broke down. But as I drove away, tears blurring the road in front of me, I knew it was the only way. I couldn't risk my family's life. It was better for it to happen when I was alone. It was less risky that way.

I didn't have a destination. I just drove and drove for hours on end, expecting the worst at every turn. I went out of the city and onto the highway as the sun set around me. At one point, I looked at the clock. 11:43 pm. Any moment now, it would be over.

As I drove, I found myself returning to thoughts that I had long since locked away. In those final minutes, I thought of Cameron. Was this what my brother felt in the moments before his death? Was he this scared? Did his heart hurt this much? Or did he pass quickly and painlessly? I prayed for the latter. I wouldn't have wished what I was feeling on anyone in the world.

When the clock hit 11:55 pm, I couldn't drive anymore. I pulled over on the side of the highway, unable to keep the panic at bay any longer. The edges of my vision were blurred, darkening from lack of oxygen. I clutched my hands in front of me, desperate to stop their shaking as I felt each second slip by.

11:56.

11:57.

At any point now, one of the cars would hit mine. The engine would explode, I would get struck by a rogue bullet. At any moment, something would happen to end my life. My heart beats punctuated my thoughts.

I *beat* am *beat* going *beat* to *beat* die.

11:58.

11:59.

My heart was pounding in my ears, so loud that it drowned out everything else around me. I could feel it growing harsher and more irregular. There was no air left to breathe. My vision was almost completely black and I struggled to see my own hands in front of me.

And that's when it happened.

———

"Cassidy ..."

Someone was calling my name. From where, I couldn't tell. It seemed to be from all around me, in no particular direction.

"Cassidy, wake up."

My eyes blinked open and I realized I was standing. I wasn't sure how that was possible, because everything around me was gray. No floor, no ceiling; just a single color. And there I was in the middle of it, somehow standing.

Standing, but not alone.

In front of me was a face that had haunted my memories, a face that at one point I had convinced myself I had imagined. But there he was, in front of me, looking like not a day had passed between our last meeting.

"There you are," Lou whispered, grinning at me the same way he had eleven years prior. "Hello again, Cassidy."

I looked around at the nothingness, then back to him. "Am I ... dead?"

He nodded. "To be honest, I was getting a little worried toward the end. You were taking your time going out."

As I began to come to my senses, I quickly realized what was so out of place about all of this. "What are you doing here?"

"I think you know the answer to that already."

My eyes crept across his smile, the darkness of his eyes. There was something different about him. I had felt it all those years ago, but it was even stronger now. He wasn't who I first thought he was. "Who are you?" I whispered.

His smile grew wider, teeth sharp and shining. "Who do you think I am?"

Who was he? He was Lou, one of the people from the grief session I went to. But ... was he? Had I actually seen him at the therapy center, or did he just *tell* me that I did? What was he doing here, at the end of my life? As I mulled over the questions, one solution rose to the forefront of my mind. I couldn't say it, couldn't speak the name. But when he smiled, I knew he had read my mind. And he had confirmed my worst fear.

*Lou was short for ...*

"I don't understand." The words shook as they passed my lips. "Why did you ..."

"Choose to help you?" he finished for me, then shrugged. "I knew you were after something. And I knew I could tell you what you wanted to know."

My gaze dropped to stare at the grayness beneath me. "So it happened, just like it was supposed to."

I was surprised to hear him laugh. "Well, not *exactly* like it was supposed to."

I looked up. His eyes were dark and cold, completely void of emotion or light. "What do you mean?"

"Humans are all the same. You'll believe anything I tell you." He shook his head at me like a parent scolding a child. "You were never going to die on November 18th, Cassidy."

Even though there was no air in my lungs, I felt like I was choking. "W-what?"

"Of course I don't have that kind of knowledge. There's only one who does and He doesn't exactly make house calls."

I tried to wrap my head around what he was saying, what his words *meant*. "But if I wasn't going to die, why did you tell me November 18th?"

"Because you wanted a date." He relished every word, running his eyes over the pain contorting my expression. "You're all so desperate to know more than you should. You look into the stars, searching for answers, or read your daily horoscope to hear how your day will be. It's all so generic and means nothing, but suddenly, when it's *your* sign, it means something. You *make* that prediction a reality. If the little free cookie that comes with your Chinese food says you're going to be disappointed, suddenly everything that comes your way seems lackluster. If the magazine tells you today is going to be your best day this week, the world becomes brighter. It works for mood, the outcome of your day ..." He gave me a knowing smile. "It even works for the day you die."

My unbeating heart sank. "I was never going to die on November 18th?"

He shook his head. "Nope."

"But ... then why did I?"

"Because you thought you were. Just like every other human on this planet, you craved power and control over your life. You would rather make something horrible come sooner than it had to than not know when it was coming at all." He narrowed his eyes at my confused expression before adding, "You gave yourself a heart attack, Cassidy. *You* caused your death that night. If you hadn't believed me for all those years, you'd still be alive with Austin and Emma."

If I could still cry, I knew there would be tears flowing down my face. But the dead don't cry, so I just stood there. "What did —" I swallowed, tried again. "What was the trade for? You never told me."

Lou narrowed his gaze. "You know exactly what you owe." And staring into his black eyes, feeling the heaviness of the weighted soul in my chest, I did. A moment of silence passed. Then he held out a hand. "Come, Cassidy. It's time."

I stepped forward. In my mind, I held my last moments with Austin and Emma. But even the memory of their faces couldn't bring me comfort now that I was staring eternity in the face. I took his hand.

And then I was really, truly gone.

*Fear is not something to be frightened of. It is not something to run or hide from. It is something to be embraced, to be expected. If we do anything to try and lessen its chill, it will inevitably control us. But all is not lost, not yet. There is still time to change, to control that which controls us.*

*So if you take nothing else from this collection of tales,*
*take away this:*
*Embrace your fear*
*and live on.*

# Acknowledgements

I wrote this collection more for myself than any of my other books. I knew the subject matter would be difficult, that it would challenge me past anything that I had done before — but these stories demanded to be written. It wasn't easy and there were some days I considered putting the project down because of how vulnerable I had to be in order to write the way I needed to. In the end, though, the satisfaction I feel by putting these long-held emotions (and fears) into words made all those sleepless nights well worth it. That being said, this collection might never have made it into the world had it not been for the following people:

To my dear parents, thank you for not sending me to therapy immediately after you read the first draft of this collection. You more than anyone understand what these stories mean to me and that I'm not crazy, just a writer with an overactive imagination and a love of the macabre. I cannot thank you enough for the undying enthusiasm and support you have for my work. It means more to me than you know.

As for the rest of my family, I'm sorry if I disturbed any of you or gave you nightmares. It's no secret that I like spooky stuff and I didn't hold anything back for this collection. You're welcome! Crina, your work is absolutely incredible. It's been amazing working with you and I wish you the best in whatever comes next on your artistic journey. You've done so much to enhance this collection and I can't thank you enough.

High school friends who have been with me since the beginning, thank you for continuing to stay by my side. You've seen me at my best and worst and I am forever grateful that you stuck with me through it all.

To my new-found college friends, I'm beyond thankful that I met each and every one of you. Meeting you turned what could've been some of the hardest times into some of my best memories. I cannot wait to see where life takes us next and I'm so glad you're with me for the ride. Special thanks to Sydney, Sarah, Corey, Bobby, Pam, Lizzy, Bryan, Sam, Ian, Marcus, Spencer, Gerard, Genesis, and Chris!

Beta readers: thank you for tearing this book apart (in the kindest way possible)! I am so appreciative of the time and energy you put into making A Weighted Soul the best it could be. I understand how crazy college can be and it truly means a lot that you would give up your precious study and sleep time to read my work. I will make it up to you in cheap ramen noodles because that's all I can afford.

Every year, I meet more amazing people in the online author community. I am so glad that I get to share my love of writing and storytelling with all of you and I can't wait to see what all of you accomplish next on your writing journeys. Shout out to Zachary James, Mandi Lynn, Kristen Martin, Bethany Atazadeh, Meg LaTorre, Jenna Moreci, and Lauren Redwood!

And how could I forget all the wonderful people who tune into my YouTube videos and online content? I cannot express how thankful I am that you take the time to watch and appreciate what I create. I love you guys!

To all the people who have inspired me in ways big and small, you're a part of this book as well. Some of your influences are more obvious than others. Some of you may not even realize that I'm writing about you. Either way, you are a part of A Weighted Soul.
I thank God for helping me utilize my gift in this creation and St. Francis de Sales for the prominent role he's played in my life. Veritas!

Finally, I thank you. If you're reading this book, you've inspired me to bring Cassidy, Francesca, James, Rosalee, and all the others onto paper. Storyteller, in my opinion, is one of the greatest titles one can hold. But the stories cannot be told if there is no one to listen.

# ABOUT THE AUTHOR

J. L. Willow voraciously read everything she could get her hands on as a child and continues to this day. She was inspired by the way words on a page could capture the imagination, beginning her journey as a writer at just six years old. When she's not holding a pencil or a book, she can be found belting her favorite musicals or studying to become a mechanical engineer. Days off are spent relaxing with her family in New Jersey. She is also the author of the contemporary crime novel *The Scavenger* and the paranormal thriller *Missing Her*.

WWW.JLWILLOW.COM

# ABOUT THE ILLUSTRATOR

Crina Magalio is a published book illustrator, digital illustrator, and pet portrait artist. Her expressive illustrations are drawn by hand, inked, and colored digitally. She earned her Bachelor of Fine Arts degree in Illustration from the Maryland Institute College of Art in 2018. One of her science fiction narrative illustrations was included in the internationally published Penguin Random House book *Doctor Who: Illustrated Adventures*. Crina's short story "Beasley's London Adventure," featuring her original animal characters, is a work in progress.

She eagerly continues to work with local NJ authors J. L. Willow and Dan Meyer. Crina's first book illustrations can be found in Dan Meyer's children's book *It All Started With A Chickadee*, a story about the importance of sharing.

Currently, Crina is excited to showcase new illustrations for Dan Meyer's story "Hello Good Buy," to be released in 2021. Crina hopes that J. L. Willow's readers will suspend their disbelief as they immerse themselves in the suspenseful stories and mysterious illustrations!

www.ingramcontent.com/pod-product-compliance
Lightning Source LLC
Chambersburg PA
CBHW021700110726
47902CB00007B/2005